Children of
Cain
A Vampire Omnibus

A.S.Chambers

[handwritten inscription: To Danni Farrar, All the best! O.S.Chambers]

This edition published in 2019.
Copyright © 2019 Basilisk Books.
High Moon, Nightingale and Girls Just Wanna Have Fun first published in Oh Taste And See © 2014 A.S.Chambers
First Hunt – Then and First Hunt – Now first published in All Things Dark And Dangerous © 2015 A.S.Chambers
Family, Visions And Prophecies and Dark Justice Prologue first published in Let All Mortal Flesh © 2016 A.S.Chambers
Memento first published Mourning Has Broken © 2018 Basilisk Books

A.S.Chambers asserts his moral right to be identified as the author of this work.

Cover art © 2018 Liam Shaw Illustration.

ISBN: 978-1-9999655-6-3

DEDICATION

For Bram Stoker, Stephen King and Anne Rice.
Without their inspiration, I would not be where I am today.

ALSO BY A.S.CHAMBERS:

Sam Spallucci Series.
The Casebook of Sam Spallucci - 2012
Sam Spallucci: Ghosts From The Past - 2014
Sam Spallucci: Shadows of Lancaster – 2016
Sam Spallucci: The Case of The Belligerent Bard – 2016
Sam Spallucci: Dark Justice - 2018
Sam Spallucci: Troubled Souls – Due 2019
Sam Spallucci: Bloodline – Due 2020

Short Story Anthologies.
Oh Taste And See – 2014
All Things Dark And Dangerous – 2015
Let All Mortal Flesh – 2016
Mourning Has Broken – 2018
Hide Not Thou Thy Face – Due 2019

Novellas.
Song Bird - Due 2019

Ebook short stories.
High Moon - 2013
Girls Just Wanna Have Fun - 2013

Contents

ACKNOWLEDGEMENTS

For avid reader, Ann Daniel, for providing the inspiration for this book's awesome cover and for the vastly talented Liam Shaw for making it a reality.

Foreward

Vampires.

I think it's safe to say that if it wasn't for the blood-sucking denizens of the night, I would never have started writing.

I was a prolific early reader, borrowing multitudes of books from my local library from the early age of three. However, by about the age of ten, I had drifted away from reading — the reason being a dearth of material for pubescent boys. It was all Enid Blyton and such and I was just not a lashings of ginger beer kind of kid.

It wasn't until I picked up an abridged copy of *Dracula* in my high school library that I realised that there were actually things out there which interested me again. And these things lurked in the shadows of our imagination. They were the werewolves, the ghosts, the unnamed monsters, but especially they were the vampires.

I think, initially, it was the lure of never growing old and never getting ill that first drew me in. As those of you who have read *The Casebook of Sam Spallucci* and *Sam Spallucci: Shadows of Lancaster* will probably know, my father was crippled with debilitating rheumatoid arthritis and I explored this and his resulting death in the aforementioned books. All I knew of old age was that you withered, you wasted and you died. The thought of superhuman powers and life immortal was, to an idealistic teenage carer, something to aspire to.

So, after the abridged *Dracula*, came the full, luxuriously rich version. After that came *Salem's Lot.* Then, something which turned my whole concept of the vamps upside down. Anne Rice's vampire chronicles. The world of Lestat, Louis, Armand and all those vivid characters had me gripped. They weren't just *super*human; they were *totally* human. They portrayed themselves as these superior beings who were so much better than us but, not so deep down, they possessed the same character flaws that they had owned as mere mortals. They were subject to love, anger, pride, jealousy and, bizarrely, a fear of death. One of the images that still remains with me is from *The Queen of The Damned* where one of the vampires dies and is seen floating up into a purgatorial nothingness.

So it was that, as a teenager, I started writing my own stories which were, in essence, fan fiction.

3

I created my own vampire, named Claw, who would be a force for good. He roamed a distant future where the world that we knew had perished and all modern niceties and extravagancies were removed. This vampire was hunting down creatures that served a mysterious master known as Kanor and they preyed on the fragile remnant of humanity. The Divergent Lands were born.

Sam Spallucci was created around the same time, rather notoriously in the back of a dull Chemistry lesson, but it wouldn't be for over twenty years until his world and the world of the vampires would blend together in the as yet unpublished *Fallen Angel*. Even then, it still wasn't until *The Case of the Vexed Vampire* appeared in *The Casebook of Sam Spallucci* in 2012 that the two were firmly cemented together.

Since then, my *shadowy policemen* have developed and evolved. Like most of this universe that I am creating, I know exactly where they are headed and how things will pan out and end for all the characters, just as each of them know how they will eventually die. This intimate knowledge of one's own death was something that came to me from nowhere. It struck me as the ultimate slap in the face by fate: you can have all this strength, longevity and youth, but you will be constantly thinking, "Is today the day? Will this be my last?" I think it is what grounds my vampires in reality and makes them truly relatable to us mere mortals. They all react differently. Nightingale throws herself into the role as mother; Marcus bears his burden heavily as a protector of his queen; Tigress is out to live life to the fullest; Scorpion tags along with her true love whilst feeling the increasing burden of her prophetic gift; Dave... well we shall just have to wait and see what happens there...

A quick word about the stories.

The Justice shorts are mainly set over a period of just a few days in the Wild West of America. They follow the young vampire who is still struggling to come to terms with his new role in the supernatural world. Unable to fully tear himself away from his mortal past, he adopts an orphan boy before being reunited with his vampire family. The fourth tale in this section was a short taster prologue for *Sam Spallucci: Dark Justice*. It appeared alongside *Family* in my third short story anthology *Let All Mortal Flesh*. This snippet brings Justice crashing into the modern world and gives us a glimpse of what he has been up to since we last saw him.

The Dave and Nightingale stories ran concurrently with the Justice stories in my first three anthologies. Together, they flesh out the characters that we had first encountered in *The Case of the Vexed Vampire*. They also serve to fill in some mythology and history regarding the Children of Cain and pave the way for the fourth Sam Spallucci novel: *Dark Justice*.

I have stated many times that Scorpion and Tigress are probably my two most favourite

5

characters in my books. They are a complete Yin and Yang. Tigress is the volatile free spirit, whereas the silent Scorpion is there to temper her partner's explosive and unpredictable nature. This is seen perfectly in *Memento*, which is my personal favourite story in this omnibus. It is interesting to see how my writing style has developed (hopefully for the better...) since I wrote *Girls Just Wanna Have Fun* back in 2012 (the same year that I penned *High Moon*).

Anyway, my vampires truly are my children. I have watched them grow from infancy to some of the most developed, well-rounded characters in Sam's universe. For those of you who have already read these stories, I hope that sitting down with my children once again will make you smile once more or even, at times, cry. For those of you for whom this is your first accompaniment with the Children of Cain, sit back, fasten your seat belt and enjoy the ride.

ASC 2019.

Justice

High Moon

The young boy huddled up against the splintery decaying barrels in a vain attempt to shelter from the bitter chill of the night-time air. He scraped his tattered rags tight as his limbs juddered involuntarily. It had not always been like this.

Once, there had been a house.

Once, there had been a father.

Once, there had been warm, satisfying food filling his belly.

Once, a mine had thrived in Salem.

Now there was just the harsh, unforgiving cold.

Sleep refused to grant him merciful release, so he sat and watched the others on the platform. The guard, dusty and pompous, patrolled his small realm, occasionally glancing at the cracked clock as it clunked the long, cold minutes away. An old-timer sat on a bench, gripping his wooden cane —

blind to the desolate reality that surrounded him, his enfeebled mind captured by the memory of glory days long past. Then there was the mangy old mutt that kept itself to itself and scavenged from the scraps of those who passed it by, with or without a swift kick.

The boy felt the wooden barrels start to tremble and glanced up at the ancient clock. The large finger was nearing the top and the small digit was off to the left. The night train was approaching.

Only two trains stopped at Salem these days: the day train and the night train. The day train took those who wished to escape and the night train was invariably empty.

No one ever actually came to Salem – no one in their right mind, anyways.

The vibrations intensified and the boy saw the locomotive chugging into view — its thick plumes of steam churning up into the night sky, drifting past the sallow face of the Hunter's Moon. The gigantic wheels started to clatter on the iron tracks and a whistle shrieked. The guard took his customary position at the head of the platform — his thumbs tucked in his tired, old waistcoat; the drab, brown material of which had seen far more resplendent days in the man's youth, but was now just another testament to the death and decay that enveloped the terminally afflicted town.

Slowly, wearily the train rolled in, trundling to a grinding halt — gears and pistons groaning like an elderly spinster rising from a wicker chair. Then, as the steam and smoke dissipated, something quite unexpected happened in the light of the full moon. A door swung lazily open and a boot stepped down onto the grimy platform. The boy shifted for a better view of this unlikely occurrence.

There was a soft thunk as another boot joined the first, and the boy caught sight of the disembarking passenger. He stood tall and erect, a long black coat trailing down to just above his shiny, immaculately polished boots and a flat, wide-brimmed hat secured firmly on his head.

All feelings of hunger and cold fled into the dissipating steam of the giant behemoth that began to growl and churn its way back into the night. This truly was something to behold. A stranger had come to Salem! The boy watched enrapt as the stranger slung his gunny sack over his broad shoulder and turned to peer down the platform. The young lad gasped as the man's eyes lit on him for an instant before moving on to the old-timer. He felt as if someone had taken a good, long look deep inside his heart and seen every bad, wicked thought he had ever known — like the time he had wished the owners of the mine dead for shutting the pit and moving out of town, leaving his father with no income and the table with no food.

They were dark eyes, so dark. The boy had never seen the like of them before. Or was it just that the man's narrow face was so pale in contrast? The boy knew not nor cared not as he hastily scrabbled round behind the barrel and listened above the sound of his beating heart to the slow footsteps of the stranger walking over to where the blind man sat.

The boots came to a solid halt and a voice as dry as the desert wind asked, "Where will I find your sheriff?"

The old timer mumbled something unintelligible from behind his grizzled beard and the stranger waited patiently for a few heart beats before turning and walking over to the barrels where the young boy crouched, quaking in his rags.

Clunk, clunk they walked across the platform. Foot after sure foot. No hesitation, no fear. Purpose filled every footfall until they stopped just a few feet away and there was total silence.

The boy closed his eyes in terror and tried not to whimper. He had never been so scared in all his life. This man was Death. He had to be. Something foul and vicious emanated from him. The boy could feel tears starting to well behind his eyes and he was sure he would pee himself when, out of the blue, something plopped down into his lap.

He screamed and bolted forward as the object rolled onto the dirty floor.

"First time I've ever seen anyone scared by an apple," came the rasping voice of the stranger.

The boy opened his eyes and looked at the fruit lying in the shadows, then up at the face of the man peering down over the barrels. He seemed to be smiling and all the dark emotions he had exuded before had dissipated. The boy's stomach growled and he snatched up the green fruit, gave it a quick polish and bit in hungrily.

The stranger nodded appreciatively and perched himself on one of the barrels, quietly watching the boy devour the sweet-tasting fruit. When every last succulent morsel had vanished, the man enquired, "Now your stomach is full, perhaps you can tell me where the sheriff's office is?"

The boy nodded. How could he have been so mistaken by this kind man? He could feel nothing but warmth and friendship rolling off him now. He gave the same feeling as the sun did when one stretched out under its warm rays on a summer's day.

"It's on the main road through the centre of town, sir," volunteered the boy, wiping apple juice from his dirty chin with the heel of his grubby hand, "opposite the saloon. But you won't find anyone there at this time of night."

The man's smile faded and, once more, ice writhed its way into the boy's stomach, causing the undigested apple to somersault.

"There'll be someone there, lad," the stranger growled. "They're expecting me." With that, he spun on his boot heel and walked over towards the steps at the end of the platform.

The boy manoeuvred out from behind the barrels and watched the stranger disappear around the corner of the station. Suddenly there was an emptiness in his stomach that even the juiciest fruit could not fill. This man was different. He had a purpose. What that purpose was, the boy was unsure of, but he was darned if he was going to sit shivering here in the cold night air when he could be finding out. He scampered after him, his bare feet slapping against the dusty wooden boards of the platform, and paused at the edge of the building to peer around the corner. True to his word, the man was heading straight up the main street towards the centre of town, where the outline of the sheriff's office sat square and squat opposite the saloon and the general store.

The boy grimaced. The sheriff was a spiteful man by the name of Carson. He had not been elected to the post, but had seized it three years ago when the vacancy had arisen following the untimely death of its previous occupant. Carson had been a stranger to town having ridden in just a few weeks previous. No one knew anything about his history, but rumours abounded. Some said that he had come from back east and had left a trail of blood in his wake. Some said that he was in the pay of the now defunct mining corporation. Some said that he was a gunslinger who had gone bad and had decided to fashion his own little kingdom in this backwater parish.

Whatever his history, whatever his aim, the boy knew one thing: Carson would not like being troubled at this time of night. The man was meaner than a hungry rattle snake and twice as poisonous. He had surrounded himself with toadies who, when they weren't out implementing his own cruel brand of law-making, sat around outside the saloon leering at the women-folk and jeering at those with no strength to stand against them.

"Carson!"

The stranger's hard voice broke the boy's reverie.

"Carson! I'm here! Come and face me! Justice has come to Salem this night!"

For a short while there was nothing, not even the sound of an insect or a night bird, but the stranger stood expectantly outside the sheriff's office, his hands loose by the side of his long black coat.

The boy's curiosity urged him forward and he scurried down the edge of the street, desperate not to be observed, sliding under the raised footpath in front of the general store. He shuffled on his belly through dust and dirt until he gained a wide view of the street. Then, just as he hunkered down to watch the show, the sheriff's door swung open and three deputies sauntered out, spreading into a thin line, facing the stranger.

The boy felt the atmosphere in the street was akin to how the weather seemed just before a wild storm raged in from the desert. It was charged with expectant excitement. Hell was about to break loose and there would be casualties.

"You shouldn't a come here," called out one of the deputies. "This here's a quiet town."

The stranger stood silent, his hands still loose by his side, his face fixed on the three men.

"What's the matter?" shouted another deputy. "Can't you talk?"

The boy saw the stranger's shoulders rise and fall in his long, dark overcoat. He looked from one to the other of the men facing him and said quietly but clearly in the still night air, "You men do not concern me. Walk away and there will be no blood shed here tonight." He lowered his gaze to the street floor in front of him, apparently content to just study a small stone that was impacted in the road's dusty surface.

First there was silence, then there was a bray of laughter. "You sure got some balls, stranger," the first deputy mocked. "There's three of us and only one of you. The only blood likely to be shed is yours."

His fellows joined in the rough, callous laughter which echoed through the empty street until the stranger did one simple thing: he looked up from the stone he had been studying in front of his highly polished boot.

In the dim light, the boy could see the danger in his dark, shadowed eyes. So too could the unwise deputies and one of them made for his gun, swiftly followed by the others. Shots rang out — the boy could not tell how many — and the acrid perfume of lingering gun-smoke hung in the cool night air.

The stranger still stood exactly where he had before — unmoved, uninjured.

The boy's eyes were almost as wide as those of the deputies. This was unbelievable! He had clearly been shot a number of times, as scorched, bloodied holes in his clothes bore witness, but he was not even betraying as much as a slight sway to his stance.

The three deputies stood aghast, their guns wavering in their undecided grips. They were clearly at a loss.

Then three distinct shots rang out and the three men dropped down, dead.

The boy swung his eyes back from the bloody corpses — which now all bore three precise head shots — to the stranger who remained standing in exactly the same fashion, the only difference being that a vague pall of gun-smoke now encircled him.

The boy gave an involuntary squeak and the stranger spared him a glance before calmly striding over to the warm corpses and inspecting his handiwork with the point of his boot. He sighed sadly before raising his head, closing his eyes and breathing in deep of the dead air.

There was a muffled crashing noise as something was either dropped or fell over in the sheriff's office.

At once the gunslinger's eyes shot open and his head snapped towards the municipal building. Then he was a blur, a streak of black crashing through the solid wooden door.

The boy scrambled along under the raised walkway for a better look at what was going on. There were more crashes which were accompanied by shouts and followed by an almighty scream as the sheriff came flying backwards through the ground floor window, pieces of splintered wood and smashed glass cascading alongside him onto the street.

The heavy-set man, rolled and clawed his way to his feet. He shouted and swore in a tremulous high voice at the sight of his dead deputies as he fumbled for his gun. The watching boy cringed. He knew it would be hopeless for the man.

As the stranger emerged steadily out of the broken doorway, the sheriff fired off shot after panicky shot. Some may have hit the impervious hunter, some may have just gone wide — the boy could not tell. All he was sure of was that the sheriff was as dead as his deputies.

"Carson!" roared the stranger as he stalked his way down onto the dusty street, "Your time here is finished. I have come for you, you abomination!"

Carson panic-stricken shifted frantically from side to side, saw there was no help coming from the town he had righteously screwed for the last three years, threw his useless gun at the stranger and made a break for it.

At least, he tried to.

The stranger leapt off his feet and glided through the air with his black coat flapping bat-like behind him. He descended on the back of the fleeing sheriff, dropping him to the floor like a hungry cougar downing a stricken buffalo.

"Justice is served," hissed the stranger, then threw back his head before seeming to ram his face down onto Carson's neck. The boy frowned. All he could see from his low vantage point was the rear of the stranger with his shoulders hunched over in his long coat.

But he could hear.

He could hear all too well.

Carson was screaming. He was shrieking and begging for his life. First there was shouting and cursing, then there was pleading, then pure unadulterated terror followed by pathetic, weakened whimpers.

Then there was silence.

The silence was the worst of all.

When he had finished the deed, whatever it had been, the stranger stood up straight and brushed himself down. Piqued curiosity was getting the better of the boy once more, and he emerged from his hiding place for a better look. The stranger was covered in a fine powdery substance that looked for all intent and purposes like dried clay. The boy frowned then gasped when he saw the remains of Sheriff Carson.

All that was left were his clothes and the withered, powdery remnant of a cadaver.

The boy tentatively approached the desiccated form and gingerly prodded the skull with his finger. His stomach lurched as the dry, fragile skull collapsed under his touch.

He turned and an unspoken question formed on his lips.

"You don't want to know," the stranger said in no more than a whisper. He suddenly seemed tired, weary — as if he had just exerted himself to a great extent. He turned on his heel and began to walk away.

"Wait!" called out the boy.

The stranger stopped but did not turn.

"Who will be our sheriff now? You?"

Another sigh shrugged the shoulders of the black coat. "Not me."

"Then who?"

The stranger walked over to his gunny sack, picked it up and said, "That is for all of you good people to decide," before continuing to walk off to the edge of town. "I have to find somewhere where I can rest now. Somewhere," he paused as if searching for the word, "undisturbed."

The boy glanced around the street that was empty of all life except for himself and the stranger. All he had for company was four corpses. No one else had come to investigate the gun-shots and screams. Not even a curtain had flickered.

He was all alone.

The stranger had reached the point where the main street met the edge of the town. He stood pondering his options under the Hunter's Moon which had now begun its descent towards the horizon.

"I know of a place that might suit you," the boy called after the stranger.

The curious man turned and his eyes bored into the youngster with interest.

"A cave not far from here," the boy continued, walking up to the stranger. "It is very private. I could take you."

"Once you walk with me, there would be no turning back. You realise that, don't you?" The gunslinger's voice was doleful, yet the boy could sense there was just a trace of hope in there.

The youngster nodded.

So did the stranger.

No more words passed between them as they walked out into the desert and left the town behind them.

First Hunt - Then

The small fire crackled in the hollow pit that had been roughly dug in the rocky floor of the small cave. The boy shivered as he rubbed his hands together in a vain attempt to draw some heat from the puny flames that danced languidly in the cold night air. He glanced over at the tall silhouette that was framed in the opening to the cave.

No shivers over there.

No sign of discomfort whatsoever.

The dark form just stood, a black statue looking out over the scrub and the surrounding plains. What was it watching? The boy had no idea, nor did he care. Right now he cared about just one thing.

His stomach rumbled loudly.

The silhouette moved as the figure turned to regard the boy. "Are you hungry?" it asked.

The boy nodded. "Yes. Thirsty too."

"When did you last eat?" The voice was deep and dry, like a sandstorm rushing in from a distance, ready to consume an unsuspecting village.

The boy trembled. "When you gave me an apple."

The figure cocked its head to one side. "Was that not two days ago?"

The boy nodded vigorously.

"Why have you not eaten since?" asked the voice, truly perplexed.

"I was afraid to ask."

The silhouette broke form as the man (if the boy could call him that) bent down towards the youngster. The flames of the fire flickered warmly in his worried eyes. "Never be afraid of me. I would never, ever harm you. Understand?"

The boy nodded once more. He felt the churning of dread in the pit of his stomach settle down as something akin to an emotional blanket swathed his tired body. He smiled up into the eyes of his saviour, the one who had whisked him away from a life of destitution and poverty to one of...

Well, he was not sure what yet, but he knew it would be better than it had been.

The man smiled back at him. "Let's go find you something to eat."

The man that was not a man cursed himself in the silence of his mind: Stupid. Stupid. Stupid. How could he have been so forgetful? Had it really been two days since he had eradicated the construct vermin in the town of Salem? He sighed. His concept of time and mortal matters was becoming somewhat less than tangible with every day.

Perhaps that was why he had let the boy come with him? He was a tenuous grasp on day-to-day reality.

He looked down at the small chap. How old was he? Ten? Eleven? He was so malnourished; it was hard to tell. His tattered clothes hung on him like rags and his bare feet scuffed the dust as they walked out onto the plains.

The creature that looked like a man but whose heart did not beat and lungs did not breathe suddenly found himself somewhere else. A happier time where another young boy skipped idly beside him, carrying over his shoulder a fishing rod that was longer than he was tall. They were off to catch some fish for their supper from the creek near their house. The boy's mother was at home setting the table and preparing water with which to cook their meal.

"What's wrong?"

The boy of now spoke and dragged the man that was not a man back to the present.

"Nothing."

The boy pointed upwards. "You have something on your face."

He rubbed the heel of his hand against his cheek and it came away smeared red with the blood of a single tear. "It's nothing," he reassured his young companion. "Nothing at all." He took the family snapshot, the final moment before his world had died, and locked it up securely in the strongbox of his subconscious. "So have you ever been hunting before?"

The boy shook his head. "No, sir. My dad thought I was too young."

"Really?" The man raised an eyebrow and muttered something quietly about modern youth being treated as soft as a whore's caress. "So you've never fired a gun?"

The boy shook his head as a heavy killing machine was pressed into his small hand.

"It's easy," came the abridged explanation. "Point that end at the thing you wish to eat and pull the trigger."

"Wh...what if I miss?"

"You go hungry."

He watched the boy hold the pistol as if it were going to turn around and bite him, then sighed deeply. "Perhaps we ought to try using a snare instead?"

Half an hour later, the two hunters were skulking behind a small, scrub-covered mound that overlooked a snare set carefully where the older of the two knew a rabbit would run. His sharp eyes could see small disturbances in the dusty ground that had been caused by the scampering of rabbits and his nose could detect the scent of at least two lingering lagomorphs. He crouched quietly under the night sky, his limbs unaffected by the need to remain motionless and still.

Next to him, the boy fidgeted.

He ignored the disturbance.

The boy fidgeted again.

Still, he ignored it.

The boy coughed.

Without moving his eyes from the rabbit run, the man said, "Do you really want to eat?"

"My legs ache."

"Worse than your stomach?"

"No."

"Then ignore them."

Quietly, the boy shifted position until he was lying on his front, peering through the scrub. "So how does it work, again?"

"The rabbit bounces happily through the thicket as it usually does; the wire catches around its neck and kills it."

"Kills it?"

"Yes."

"How?"

"It restricts the flow of blood to the brain and the rabbit suffocates."

The boy leaned back and looked aghast at his teacher. "That's awful! It's so cruel!"

"Keep your voice down," the man hissed. "You'll startle the rabbits."

"And that's worse than throttling them?"

"It is if you want to fill that bottomless pit of yours."

The boy sank down against the small hillock and folded his arms across his chest. "Well, I don't like it," he pouted.

The man let his face sink into the dusty earth. Was this what eternity had planned for him? "Do you like being hungry more?" he snapped, then immediately regretted the harshness of his tone when he lifted his head and saw the boy's face crumple. "Oh, no. Wait. I'm sorry... I didn't mean to..." His voice faltered as the young lad threw himself into his arms and sobbed.

They had given up on rabbit. By the time that the boy had gained control of his emotions, the fluffy meals had long since scarpered. Instead, they had decided to make their way to the next town. The boy did not know what its name was, but he knew that it was not too far. His late father had taken him there for supplies a few times when he was younger.

As they walked along the dusty track, the boy appeared to be pondering something.

"What's on your mind, Son?"

"What's your name?"

The man raised an eyebrow without even breaking stride. He had been expecting this question sooner or later, this one and another.

He did not want to have to answer the other one just yet.

"Justice."

"Is it biblical?"

"Pardon?"

"My dad used to say that names oughta be biblical or they weren't proper names."

"Well, there's lots of justice in the Bible."

"Why did your folks choose it?"

"They didn't. I did."

The boy stopped in his tracks. Justice carried on walking, feeling the subtle change in air patterns as the boy's mouth hung open in shock. "You chose your own name?"

"Yes. When I started out doing what I do."

There was the scampering of bare feet as the boy caught up with him. "You mean like killing bad'uns?"

"You could put it like that."

They walked in silence for a while. Justice could see the lights of the next settlement start to glow on the horizon. They would be there within the hour and then he would find food for the boy.

"What was he? Carson, I mean."

Justice considered his answer carefully. How to explain a war that had been waged in the shadows for as long as his kind could remember? How to tell this boy that everything he believed in was built upon a misconception that humans were the only sentient creatures that walked the planet.

"He was a monster. A *terrible* monster."

"What are you?"

What resembled Justice's heart trembled as the boy asked the question that he had not wanted to answer just yet.

"I'm a different kind of monster."

The boy thought that Stuartsville was more or less the same layout as Salem: a high street with a saloon that doubled up as a hotel, a store with a hitching post outside, a sheriff's office and a few buildings that he could not identify in the dark. He followed Justice over to the saloon. The clock tower above the sheriff's office read just short of ten o'clock so the sound of music and revelry could still be clearly heard sauntering its way out of the double swing doors.

"We'll lodge here and get you fed," the man who called himself a monster said matter-of-factly as he climbed the few stairs to the doors. The boy followed him, the wood feeling worn under his bare feet. He entered the saloon behind his companion and the doors swung shut behind them.

Silence descended as all eyes turned towards the tall stranger with the child.

The boy tugged at Justice's long coat and the man peered down at him. "Do you always have that effect?" the boy asked in a loud whisper.

There was the sound of a feminine chuckle followed by a cough and the awkward silence was broken, causing the background bar room noise to resume.

"It has been known," Justice smiled. "Sit yourself down here." He pulled a chair from under a table for the boy. "I'll get us a room."

As his companion's boots thunked their way across the floor to the bar, the boy surveyed his surroundings. The saloon seemed to contain all manner of folk, most of them sat with their friends, enjoying a drink at the end of the day. On one table he saw a very pretty lady running her fingers up the chest of a man who must have been her father, judging by the age of him, although why he had his arm around her in such a fashion, the boy could not tell. He spied an elderly couple at another table. The woman had a touch of grey hair protruding from under her white bonnet and she sat knitting whilst her bowler-hatted spouse drank carefully so as not to get whiskey in a voluminous moustache that reminded the boy of a pair of horse tails.

The boy's eyes stopped when they reached the next table. There sat three men with whom he did not think he would wish to mix. They wore rough, dusty clothes and scowls that spoke of ill intent. Also, their eyes never left Justice's back as he spoke to the landlord before turning and beckoning the boy over. "We have a room," he explained as he led the way upstairs. "It sounds basic but it should suffice. The owner will bring some food up shortly."

When they reached the top of the stairs to the landing that overlooked the bar, the boy said, "Those men were watching you."

Justice glanced out across the bar and breathed in deeply.

For a moment he stood stock still, just as he had earlier in the cave mouth, then he turned and continued along to their room. He opened the door and stood aside for the boy to enter. "Wait in here. Your food will come along presently," he instructed and made to leave.

"Where are you going?"

"I have business to attend to," the gunslinger explained and shut the door.

The boy lay back on the huge bed and belched loudly. On the tray next to him lay the carcass of a chicken, a few crumbs of bread and an empty glass. He felt as if he had eaten like a king! His belly was stretched and full, somewhat uncomfortably so. He rolled off the bed, stretched and padded around the bedroom in an attempt to aid his digestion. As he did so, he wondered where Justice had gotten to. He glanced out of the window and the clock tower told him that it had just gone midnight.

Had two hours really passed?

The onset of worry started to gnaw where the food lay in his stomach. Surely Justice should be back by now? The boy trotted over to the door and peeked out. The bar was in darkness; not a soul moved about downstairs and the lighting had been extinguished. Carefully, so as not to disturb any other residents, the boy tiptoed along the landing and down the stairs before heading over to the front doors. He pushed one aside and looked out into the street. As he did so, he saw the three rough-looking men turning around a corner and down an alley. He remembered the way that they had watched Justice from their table and the manner in which the gunslinger had scented the room.

Were they the same monsters like Carson?

Was Justice in trouble?

The boy made up his mind to find out and followed them, silently.

The clock tower read quarter past the hour as Justice re-entered the saloon in a foul mood. The constructs had eluded him. He had gone back down into the bar and sat waiting until they had left before following them out into his realm, the night. Then, as he had quietly stalked them through the dark, something had distracted him. There had been the softest of whispers and a new scent had drifted over on the still night air. He had stood enrapt as the smell had danced inside his nostrils and fired off certain synapses in his brain.

It had felt familiar yet new. It reminded him of a scent from the past yet was inherently different.

The hunter had shaken his head in an attempt to clear his wandering thoughts before turning and realising that his prey had vanished. Cursing silently, he had hunted in vain through the alleys of the town but had been unable to pick up the sickening smell that marked them for what they were; the new, intruding fragrance occupied his olfactory senses, blinding him to the task at hand.

In the end he had given up and returned to the saloon. Stomping disconsolately into his room, he saw just the empty bed and the remains of the devoured supper. His eyes darted round hunting for clues before he turned and ran back out faster than the human eye could observe, images from his former life rising up to haunt him once more.

The first inkling that there had been something wrong was the smell of woodsmoke, next was the drifting clouds of black that had risen over the hill from their house. He had told his son to wait in the trees where it was safe whilst he ran as fast as his mortal legs could manage back to the furnace that had once been his home. Inarticulate words had gorged their way out of his throat when he saw the lifeless body of his beautiful wife discarded on the path to their once quiet paradise. Then there had been the shrieks of fear as he had turned and seen his son being dragged out of the trees by a steel-eyed beast dressed in furs and leather.

"This brat yours?" the stranger had yelled. "Screams louder than his momma!" Then, in one swift movement he had thrown the boy to the floor and pumped two bullets in the child's head.

The man that used to be had just stood still, unable to move as the shadowy horrors of a cruel world had torn his sanctuary apart. Even when the cur had raised the gun towards him he had been

32

unable to turn and flee. Instead, he had slumped to the floor as the side of his head had exploded in agony and darkness had closed around him.

When his eyes had reopened, it had been to a whole new world. A world where his senses were heightened enabling him to achieve three important tasks:

Find the Eternals.

Protect the Twins.

Await the Divergence.

Right now, however, he was depending on these same senses to perform just one task: find the boy before the constructs did.

"Hello, Sonny," came the elderly voice. "Are you lost?"

The boy sat on a crate with his head in his hands. Some tracker he was. Within a few minutes he had lost his prey. The three rough-looking men had vanished around a corner and he had no idea where they had gone so he had sat himself down to work out his next move.

Then the elderly couple from the saloon had wandered down the alley.

"No, Ma'am," he said to the old woman in the white bonnet, "I'm just collecting my thoughts."

"In an alley?" the old man chuckled from behind his horse tail moustache. "Surely that's not a good idea at this time of night? There could be all sorts about."

"I'll be fine," the boy assured them. "I have a protector."

The elderly couple gave each other a curious look. "You mean that tall fellow you were with earlier?" asked the woman.

The boy nodded confidently.

"Funny," said the old man, his voice sounding suddenly rheumy and wet as if he had a throat full of phlegm, "but I don't see the vampire anywhere near right now."

Hairs rose on the back of the boy's neck as he slowly slid off the crate. "What did you say?" he began to ask, but the words hung quivering on his tongue as he watched stunned whilst the skin of the two old-timers started to ripple and flex under their clothes. The old man's moustache was sucked back into his face as his features sunk into a thick, brown substance that bore just a gash where his mouth should be. The woman's appearance followed suit and they lumbered towards him, their clothes sloughing off their clammy bodies to the floor.

The boy tried to run; he really did, but his feet just did not seem to want to move. Monsters: he thought to himself. *These* were the monsters. Not those men. Then the wet hand of the thing that used to be a sweet old lady that sat in saloons knitting clothes from homespun yarn clasped the youth on the shoulder and dragged him towards her ragged mouth. He squirmed at the sight of the putrid-smelling liquid trickling from the slavering orifice. It stank like a stagnant pond at the height of summer and made the boy feel like retching, but even that was not possible as fear constricted every muscle in his body.

He was aware of a deep rattling emanating from the mouth of the thing that used to be a man and realised that it was laughing, enjoying watching this young human paralysed with fear.

Then there was a noise that sounded like a boot wrenching itself out of mud and the laughing abruptly halted mid-chuckle. The boy's paralysis broke and he turned to see the monster that used to be an old man slump to the floor in two parts. Next to him stood a pretty young woman dressed in a frock coat and a small hat. In her hand was a bright, gleaming sword.

She pulled back her lips in a smile and the boy saw the sharpest teeth he could ever have imagined. In an instant she was a blur and the thing that used to be an old woman was no longer holding his hand. The well-dressed woman had the creature pinned against a wall and had plunged her teeth into its neck. There was a wet warbling noise as the thing tried to free itself but eventually the scream sounded raspy and dry as the monster turned to dust in the younger woman's embrace.

The boy heard the sound of footsteps behind him and turned to see another stranger. This one was a man, and what a man! He stood taller than Justice and his hair was a mane of bright yellow. Muscles rippled under his travelling coat as he lifted the severed remains of the other creature in his hands and rapidly drained them dry.

Just as he was becoming accustomed to the appearance of his apparent saviours, the boy felt a rush of wind and found himself whisked up into the arms of Justice. He looked up and saw relief in his companion's eyes before they tracked across the alley to the blonde giant and filled with awe.

He set the boy on the alley floor and sank down onto one knee.

"Your Majesty," said the gunslinger

The blonde man walked over with regal confidence and, taking Justice by the arm, lifted him from his genuflection.

"My son and heir," said the king, unadulterated love filling the words as he turned him to face the young woman. "Let me introduce you to your new sister."

The woman smiled prettily, her blue eyes twinkling in the night, and held out her hand.

"Hello," she said. "My name is Nightingale."

Family

The boy craned his neck to peer up at the young woman, her bright blue eyes framed by her short, dark hair. Her fancy clothes were so different to the ones that his mother used to wear. Whereas his mother's had been fashioned from fabrics that were mainly browns and greys and had consisted of more patch than original material, Nightingale's were fashioned from all manner of shiny cloths and were deep purples and reds.

"You like my clothes?"

The boy blushed and quickly studied his feet.

The sound of fresh water babbling over small, polished pebbles filled the room. The two other occupants gave a quick glance before returning to their hushed conversation.

Nightingale reined in her merriment and placed a gentle hand under the boy's chin, lifting his eyes back up to her crystal pools. "It's okay to look. I'm guessing you've not seen anything quite like us before? Well, apart from my rather dour older brother there."

The boy slipped a quick glance over to Justice, the quiet man who had rescued him from Salem just a few days previous. "About that..."

"What?" Flames from the fire danced in the young woman's eyes as she turned to prod the logs with a poker. The boy knew this was just for his benefit as the three adults had no need of the heat, being what they were.

Vampires. Undead creatures you saw pictures of in story books where they roamed the night, preying on the innocent. And yet, these three were nothing of the sort. They seemed to be on a mission, fighting other creatures, the ones made from clay. After the events in the alley, Justice had told him that those monsters were called constructs and served a dark master whose name and purpose was as yet unknown.

The boy's little world had suddenly expanded into a vast universe.

"You say that he's your brother, yet you don't look similar at all. You're all, you know, pretty," he felt himself redden again but carried on, "and he's so... so..."

"Serious?"

The boy nodded and the two of them chuckled conspiratorially in the pirouetting flicker of the fire.

"We're not kin like humans are," his new friend explained. "We just share the same father. He *created* us."

The boy looked over to the man who was talking with Justice. He was so tall! There had been large men in Salem: farmhands, miners, law-keepers. None of them, though, were the size of this individual. He was even taller than Justice, and his blonde hair flowed like a waterfall down his back. Also, when he spoke, there was an unrecognisable accent to his tongue.

"And he is your king?"

Nightingale nodded. "That he is."

"So, does that make you a princess?"

The water babbling over pebbles rolled into the room once more. "I guess it does," she smiled. "I guess it does." She leant forward and rubbed the material of his shirt between her fingers. "How long have you had this?"

The boy shrugged. "A while, I guess. I haven't gotten any new clothes since my pa died."

A cold finger stroked his cheek. "Well, I think it's about time that you did. Come on." She stood, and the boy followed her to the door. "We're just going shopping," she announced to the others. "Won't be long."

The men watched in silence as they were left behind.

"Well?" the older man asked. "What do you think?"

Justice sat back in his chair, which creaked under his weight, and raised an eyebrow. "Of my new sister?"

His king and his father nodded slowly.

"She's certainly vivacious," he smiled. "Reminds me of someone."

"A certain Briton? Or perhaps her Trojan companion?"

The gunslinger smiled. "She has the tongue of one and the insight of the other." He pondered this for a moment. "A good combination, I think. Where did you come across her?"

"England," the older man said. "She was a maid in a large house, regularly beaten and abused by her master whilst being scorned and insulted by her mistress. Now she is free." He frowned when Justice made a small noise. "Something bothering you, my son?"

The younger vampire paused as he gathered his thoughts. This was his father and his king. He needed to tread carefully out of respect. "My liege, you say that she is free. How can that be truly so?"

"What do you mean?"

"Look at us! We are creatures doomed to darkness and shadow. You as much as said so when you created me. When I cast my new eyes on my first moonrise you told me to treasure the moment as that would be the most light that I should ever encounter in my new life.

"Then you left me here."

.

The fire crackled as neither man spoke for a while.

"How can you talk of freedom," Justice continued, "when you, yourself, see yourself as nothing more than a slave? For heaven's sake, you even took that as your name – Doulos! You are a king who sees himself as just a servant."

"Mind your tongue, child." The king's voice was low but perfectly audible to his son's preternatural hearing. "You know why I chose my name. It reflects what I was and what I still see myself as. Just as yours is a snapshot of yourself. You are the lone gunslinger that roams this land, hunting down those that we seek in order to restore our world as best we can."

"As best we can..." Justice's words were quiet, thoughtful.

Doulos knew there was meaning behind them and waited for it to be forthcoming.

"I sometimes feel that we are just jabbing pins in the coyote," Justice resumed after a while. "Rather than solving the problem, we just aggravate it with each blow that we strike. Yes, we remove the construct scourge one by one, but for each we cut down, two more rise. We should be blocking the source of the poisoned stream and not desperately trying to stem the relentless flow with our undersized fingers."

The king sighed. "You know why we have to do what we do."

"We don't know who has created these creatures," Justice nodded. "Aside from vague images some have seen in dreams and nightmares, we know nothing."

"That is correct. So we continue as we do until we find this monster and sever its head from its cancer-spawning body."

"But what of the others in this world?"

The fire spat and the king cocked his head in confusion. "The others?"

"The humans? What of them? Surely we should tell them of what we do?"

The king laughed deeply. "Really? You would inform these scurrying little termites that there is in fact an eternal war being fought in their midst by two races, both of which they would find abhorrent?"

"Not all would feel that way."

"No, but the majority would. They rule their peoples with fear and aggression. Look at this land which birthed you. The European invaders slew the indigenous natives in order to steal the very ground upon which they walked. What do you think they would do if they discovered that the creatures of their fairy tales were actually real?

"They would eradicate us.

"I have no time for them."

Justice frowned. His father's words were harsh, spiteful. This disturbed him somewhat.

Doulos stood in one fluid movement. "Enough of this. Let us go out into the night and see what mischief your sister and your son are creating?"

The younger vampire rose to join the elder. "The boy is not my son. I have no desire to make him one of us."

"Really?" the king frowned as he donned his hat and his coat. "Perhaps this is why you have such a soft spot for the mortals. I advise you to be careful."

"So, what about this then?"

All the boy could do was grin maniacally as words failed to convey just how stunned he felt. In the past hour he had tried on five pairs of shoes, eight pairs of pants, numerous shirts and three jackets. His brain was whirling almost as fast as the elderly shopkeeper who was struggling to keep up with his customers' every whim of fashion.

"Well?" Nightingale pressed. "What about it?"

The latest jacket was a deep royal blue, almost black in shade. He had no idea as to what the material was but his fingers left tracks in the fibres as he stroked its soft surface.

The boy really liked it.

He nodded exuberantly.

"I think we have a winner!" the young woman declared to the shopkeeper.

The elderly man smiled benevolently, and with not a small amount of relief, as he began to bundle up the pile of clothes that his early evening shoppers had already chosen. "Will the young man want the coat packaging too?"

Nightingale looked down at the boy as he played with the fabric of the soft velvet. "I don't think we could part him from it if we tried."

The old man smiled and totted up the final bill. He did not usually open this late and had been rather cautious when the young woman had knocked insistently on his door, but it had certainly been worth it. No one ever spent this much. He handed the bill over and she placed payment on the counter. His eyes lit up at the bright, yellow gold.

"Keep the change. You've worked hard for it and that's appreciated."

The man let out a low whistle. Perhaps he would stay closed tomorrow and treat himself to a few whiskeys in the saloon? He bid the woman and her child a good night before locking the door behind them. As he slid the shutters closed, he did not notice the group of men fall into step behind his customers.

By the light of the moon, Nightingale smiled down at her young companion. He was rummaging through the parcel of newly-acquired clothes as they ambled contentedly down the street.

"Careful you don't trip," she said. "You should always look where you're going."

The boy raised his head, his grinning teeth bright in the light of the moon. "I've never had so many nice things. You've spoiled me."

"You're worth it. I know what it's like to have nothing."

"But you look all fancy."

Nightingale continued to smile, but this time the boy saw sadness in her eyes. "I wasn't always like this. I used to live a wretched life. My clothes were dull and tattered. I ate barely enough to survive. In fact, I was at death's door with a terrible illness when Doulos found me."

"How did he find you?"

The woman's eyes were off in the past as she continued her story. "He heard me singing. It was all I had left in life. I was so weak that I could not get out of my hard servant's bed. No food had been brought to me for three days and my pitcher of water had run dry. I knew that I was dying and it terrified me to the core. The thought that I would be left to rot in that miserable attic room caused me to dream nightmares of my wasted body dressed in a tattered nightgown. So I sang to myself to try and lift my spirits. My voice was frail, incredibly weak, but still he heard me. On my final night, the bedroom window slid open and he climbed in before bringing me back to life.

"Doulos saved me."

There was noise from behind and Nightingale snapped out of her reverie.

"There's no one here to save you now, my pretty." Three figures stepped out of the gloom. A strong stench of bourbon followed them. "Now why don't you just hand over those fine garments and some of your gold, then we'll be on our way."

The boy froze on the spot but next to him Nightingale just sighed. "You don't want to do this," she said in a low voice.

There was quiet then a low cackle from the three deadbeats. "Really?" the pockmarked leader continued. "Oh, but I think we do. You come into our town dressed in your fancy clothes, ordering our shopkeepers around and don't think that you'll have to pay for the privilege? Now hand the goods over!"

Nightingale shook her head. "No. We're leaving now." She placed a hand on the boy's shoulder and began to turn him away from the strangers. The boy then heard footsteps and another hand fell on his other shoulder. This one was nowhere near as gentle.

The next turn of events happened incredibly quickly.

One moment, one of the attackers was trying to drag him away; the next, the assailant was lying on the floor screaming, clutching at his arm which was now bent in a weird angle. The other two had drawn their guns and were staring ashen-faced at Nightingale who had positioned herself in front of their attackers, guarding her ward. The youth peered round her protective shield and looked up at her face then gasped when he saw what had caused the men to suddenly lose their nerve. A sharp pair of fangs were glistening in the moonlight.

"Leave us!" she hissed.

The two who still stood dragged their screaming conspirator to his feet and ran off into the night.

Nightingale and the boy watched them leave.

"Oh, we are in such big trouble," the young vampire finally admitted to the empty street.

They looked just like a pair of respectable gentlemen taking in the night air as they strolled down the main street of the western town. One wore an expensive frock coat, one a longer jacket of heavier, more practical material. Both were attired with wide-brimmed hats, suitable for keeping the sun from one's eyes on a long ride through the countryside. One sported a black cane that paced evenly as he walked. One had the unmistakable bulges of two holsters underneath his coat.

They looked as normal as normal did in this place.

Neither, however, possessed a heartbeat nor breathed in the life-giving air that sustained those who passed them. The heart of the one with the guns had stopped a few years previous and the heart of the one in the fancy frock coat had stopped many centuries before, when the world had been an entirely different place.

Different, yet curiously the same.

Technology had evolved, empires had risen and fallen. However, humanity remained ever constant: resilient, inquisitive and cruel.

Doulos had seen his fair share of cruelty. He thought back a few weeks previous to the sight of the emaciated young woman lying starving in her squalor. The reek of Death's cadaverous hand had been strikingly apparent when he had ventured into her small room. What remained of the cold, dead heart in his chest had fluttered with empathy and sorrow as he had watched her staring off into the unknown distance, softly singing to herself. He had only recently created a child. His first in his long, lonely years as a Child of Cain. He had never wanted to burden another with the responsibility with which he had been shouldered back in the days when the highest form of fashion had been a finely crafted sandal. For almost a thousand years he had walked by the side of his mother, a vampire who had seemed as old as time but was in fact just a couple of centuries older than himself.

Together they had wandered the shadows and the nights. The dull moon had been their waxing and waning guide in their hunt for the misshapen, insidious creatures of clay: constructs. They had needed to remain hidden, shrouded from the view of the humans who continued to be born, live their short lives, then die. They constantly moved from place to place so as not arouse suspicion from their natural longevity.

Never could they put down roots. Never could they befriend those who they protected.

They were outcasts. Pariahs.

He had caught the vaguely hidden glances she had cast him which told of the regret that she had carried in creating a child to lead her people upon her end.

And end she did.

One night in some Mediterranean country, Doulos had come back to the house in which they had been lodging and had found the place empty. The room had been in turmoil: furniture broken, ornaments smashed, and there had been blood.

His mother's blood.

He had tracked her to the outskirts of the village, to a clearing where a huge bonfire burned bright in the darkness of the night. In its midst was his mother, bound to a stake and roasted to a crisp. The villagers looked on, jeering and cheering as they feasted and drank the locally fermented wine.

None of them saw the sunrise of the next day.

So, when he had seen this young dying woman lying, singing quietly as her life had ebbed away, Doulos had been torn. He had not been able to let this innocent child die. Her words had been so beautiful and had told of a spotless soul, one who cared for others and saw the good in those around her. He could not let that beauty pass from this world.

Yet, what was he damning her to?

And who was responsible for her state?

He had drawn close, mesmerised by her song, and without even thinking he had drained her and fed her with his blood from which she was to be sustained. Then, as she had slept and had been reborn, he had dealt with her employers.

Their screams still echoed through his ears.

Doulos' head snapped up as did his son's. That was no distant memory. That scream was very much in the here and now.

"Trouble," he growled, and the two of them picked up their pace.

This was bad. Very bad.

"Quick, down here." Nightingale chivvied the boy down a side alley. Her first thought had been to return to the tavern and lay low until things had quietened down.

However, it appeared that their erstwhile attackers possessed a number of noisy friends and acquaintances. She pulled her young companion down behind some barrels, ignoring the stench of something rank and unmentionable, then waited for the horde to pass by, waving their torches and pitchforks or whatever it was that restless villagers used in these parts to show anger at things that they did not care to understand.

Nightingale frowned as she felt the boy quaking in fear and inwardly she cursed herself for her stupidity. "Just be quiet and they'll not notice us," she whispered reassuringly in his ear.

"We saw them come down here!" Nightingale recognised the coarse voice. It was the pockmarked leader of the little gang. "Split up and search the alleys!"

The boy froze next to her. This was not good. They needed a diversion.

"Whatever you do," she said in a low voice, "do not leave this place."

He looked up at her and her stomach lurched at the abject terror that dwelt in his young eyes.

"Stay here and you will be safe. I will lead them away and come back for you."

Nothing.

There were footsteps at the entrance to the alley.

"Please. Just nod. Anything. Tell me you understand."

The boy curled up in a ball behind the barrel.

That would have to do. There was no more time.

Nightingale erupted from their hiding place and threw herself screaming down the alley. Three villagers were left flattened on the floor as she leapt out into the main street. Heads turned to face her and shouts of surprise followed as she ran away from the crowd. Not turning around, she listened to the sound of many running feet pursuing her.

She allowed herself a small smile as she played decoy.

Two shadows silently peeled themselves away from the side of an innocuous building.

"They came down here."

Doulos inhaled through his nose and grimaced. "I'm surprised you can smell anything over the stench of sweat and horse excrement."

Justice shrugged. "I grew up in this country. Certain things are just background sensations." He followed his father out into the street. Something was wrong, and not just the angry rabble that they had been both following and avoiding for the last hour or so. Doulos was distracted. There was a matter on the king's mind that he was not sharing. "We will find them."

The older vampire nodded absentmindedly and walked off across the road.

Justice sighed quietly and followed. As he did, he was aware of another presence falling in step behind him. A quick mental dissection of aromas caused him to smile. "Greetings, sister."

"Greetings, brother," Nightingale replied.

Justice looked her up and down. "You seem somewhat dishevelled."

"Oh, you know. A late night run and all that." She grinned infectiously and walked over towards an alley which their father had just entered. "Let's get your ward and leave this place, shall we?"

"Agreed."

They both walked down into the alley and stopped when they saw Doulos peering down at some foul-smelling barrels.

There was no sign of the boy.

Nightingale screamed in surprise as she slammed into the wooden panelling that made up the wall of the alleyway. She felt herself hammered over and over again into the splintering material. In the background of her consciousness, she was aware of someone shouting, possibly at her, but things were exceptionally hazy.

Then she was free-falling onto the grimy alley floor.

Concentrating on bringing the surrounding world back into focus, she cautiously pulled herself up to her knees and looked up at an extraordinary sight. Doulos had gripped Justice by the back of his longcoat and was holding the gunslinger up above his head. Justice was ranting and raving, cursing harsh expletives which Nightingale knew instinctively were aimed at her. Tentatively, she stood up on her feet, leaning against the shattered wall for support.

"...kill her... untrustworthy... the boy..." Words started to prise apart the foggy clouds in her head and she began to comprehend what had happened.

"I'm sorry," she whispered. "I'm so sorry."

The raging vampire calmed somewhat and his father dropped him to the floor. "Enough of this," the blonde giant scowled. "What's done is done. We must leave."

His children stood and gawped as he picked up his hat, dusted down his frock coat and turned to exit the alley.

"No," said Nightingale.

"No!" shouted her brother.

Their father stopped and without turning back to them, said, "We cannot stay here. Enough damage has been done. We cannot save the boy without revealing ourselves. We must leave. Now."

There were two brief gusts of wind and he turned to view an empty alley.

"Plan?"

"Grab the boy. Leave."

"That simple?"

"That simple."

"What if anyone tries to stop us?"

Justice was silent.

Nightingale watched the growing crowd down below. The young vampires had taken the high route, silently leaping from rooftop to rooftop, providing themselves a wide perspective of the town. It had not taken them long to find the assembled lynch mob by the town hall.

The boy had to be inside.

"Well?"

"We concentrate on saving the boy then deal with anyone who gets in our way."

The younger vampire could not mistake the steel in her older sibling's voice. "No one gets hurt," she insisted. "Promise."

The gunslinger's pale eyes fixed upon her. "If anyone gets hurt, it's your fault for not protecting the boy."

"Oh, don't you go pinning this on me!" she hissed. "And why do you just call him *the boy*? Why don't you use his name?"

Justice looked away quickly.

"You are joking, aren't you? You don't know his name?"

Justice pulled out one of his six-shooters and inspected the barrel of the weapon.

"Unbelievable! You drag him away from his normal life into ours, where the monsters under the bed are real, and you don't even bother to find out his name?"

"So," Justice said, still studiously inspecting his gun, "what is it then?"

This time Nightingale was awkwardly silent.

"Perhaps you asked him when you treated him like a doll, when you were dressing him up in fine clothes? Perhaps you enquired when he sat scared in the depths of a shit-smelling alleyway?"

The female vampire just glared at her brother.

"I thought not.

"Names are funny things to our kind, aren't they? They portray what we represent rather than who we are. Is it so strange that neither of us thought to enquire of his?"

With that he leapt down into the street, guns drawn.

The first bullet took out a kneecap of an old-timer with a shotgun. The second fractured the wrist of a stable hand who fumbled with a pair of ancient pistols that he had only ever used to shoot tins off a fence. The third went harmlessly into the air and caused the rest of the crowd to scatter for shelter.

Nightingale had to begrudgingly admit to herself that she was rather impressed. She caught up with him as he reached the door to the town hall. He had his ear close to the door. "I count twelve heartbeats, one beating almost twice as fast as the others." Then, before she could answer, his foot raised and kicked the door clean off its hinges, straight into the building.

Startled cries came from within, along with the thump of two individuals being flattened by the imploding door. Four rapid shots felled four more of the mob. Nightingale sped through the gun-smoke and cracked the heads of two others.

That left three and the boy.

Two more shots. Two cries of pain. Non-fatal but excruciating.

One left.

The pockmarked assailant stood cornered in the far side of the room. The boy was grasped in front of him, his eyes as wide as a mine shaft, his fear twice as deep. A sharp knife was clasped to the child's throat.

"Give us the boy." Nightingale's voice was calm, quiet. "He comes with us. We leave," she reassured the man. "No one has died."

The mortal's eyes flickered between the two creatures in front of him. They were devils. He knew that. They stood there, tall and handsome, not a hair out of place, as if they were angels sent from on high, but he knew that they had come to drag him all the way down to the deepest, darkest depths of Tartarus.

There was no way out.

Nightingale screamed as the first drop of blood oozed from the boy's neck. The young lad's eyes seemed to fill his face as his heart beat galloped faster than a mail coach. She was aware of Justice taking aim and the gun exploding across the room followed by the insides of the killer's head decorating the wall behind him.

More and more blood soaked down the boy's blue velvet coat. The soft indigo mutated into a sticky purple as he slumped onto the floor, a pathetic gurgling bubbling up from his gizzard.

She leapt across to him and picked his limp body up in her arms. There was but one noise in the room of which she was aware. It was the dull pounding of a giant trying to climb an impossibly steep hill. Footstep after footstep became harder and harder as the incline increased. Slow and encumbered became his uneven gait until finally he stopped, sank to his knees and gave up on the futile ascent.

The woman who held the lifeless boy was incapable of words. He was gone. He had been here, but now he was gone.

And it was her fault, her own stupid fault.

"Pardon?" She had heard something. One word but it had not registered.

"Leave," repeated Justice. "Go."

"Why?" she wanted to ask, but when she looked up into his empty eyes she knew the answer. She wanted to tell him, "No," but it would be a wasted word and words were precious. You never knew when you would say your last. Each and every one had to count.

Slowly, she lay the dead boy on the blood-soaked wooden floor, rose to her feet and walked out of the room leaving ten wounded men with her grieving brother.

It was a few hours before dawn when the family was finally reunited. The Children of Cain met at a cave far away from a town in stunned mourning. Doulos had spent most of the night there before being joined by Nightingale, whose face told him all that he needed to know.

When Justice arrived, the sky was seeping from black to indigo and the weaker stars were starting to fade. As he walked towards the cave, he watched his father putting the finishing touches to a huge bonfire.

The older vampire placed his last piece of wood on the pile and turned to face his son. "There is blood on your hands," he said.

"As there is on yours," his son replied. "Mine is just fresher."

Doulos nodded. "We are what we are."

"Killers."

The older vampire placed the last of the wood on the bonfire and pushed at it to test its stability. "That we are."

"What of her?"

Doulos looked towards the cave where his son's eyes were gazing. "I don't know. I really don't."

"You think that she is different?"

The father was silent, lost in his many thoughts.

"You think she will be a better monarch than me?"

Again silence.

Justice's worried eyes glanced at the pile of wood. "Talk to me. Please, tell me what you are thinking."

"I am thinking," Doulos struck a match and tossed it onto the kindling of the pyre, "that I have seen too much death. I am thinking that I bear a secret that I can no longer hold. I could whisper it to the earth but the plants would tell all those that pass by. I could tell the sky but clouds would rain it down onto the people below. No one must know our secret, not yet. They are not ready. I cannot exist in this limbo any more.

"My child, I love you with what remains of my dead heart, just as I love your sister, but it is time for me to leave you now."

The flames pranced like plains horses in his pupils.

"But what are we to do?"

"I think you already know." With that, Doulos leapt up high and plunged into the midst of the funeral pyre.

All Justice could do was stand and watch in horror as his creator erupted into flames, like a dry cotton rag that had caught a stray spark. It was only as the fire burnt down and the ashen remains of the wood and his father fell in upon itself that he realised there was a soft sobbing coming from behind him. He turned and saw Nightingale, her face stained with blood.

"Why?"

"He could not carry on."

"Why did you not stop him?"

"I could not."

"What are we to do now?"

"You are to carry on."

"Me? What about you? Surely you are not considering…" Her eyes drifted to the dying embers.

Justice shook his head. "No. Nothing like that. I cannot be your king. I am not the right person to rule our kind. In his cold, dead heart he knew that to be the truth. That is why he created you."

Nightingale's voice rose an octave. "Me? Really? I think not. I know nothing. You are older. You have seen more. You are the first born."

"I am no ruler. I can live in the shadows but not with such a burden on my shoulders. I will do my part: furtively, silently. You will hear whispers of my deeds but you will not see me again.

"Not until the time is right.

"Our world is changing at such a rapid pace. People are not ready to know the truth yet of that which goes on right under their noses, but there will come a day when they will be ready — when they will accept that which they thought was fantasy is in fact reality. It shall be a time when I can stand in front of all the peoples of this world and tell them the truth. When that day comes, I shall return. Until then, I shall make sure that justice is served. I shall travel alone and follow my own path.

"Others of our kind will find you. They will see you for what you are: a kind, caring ruler. You shall be their Regent whilst their King is in occultation."

The first rays of the waking sun stretched their limbs above the horizon, crawling with searching fingertips across the plains. The siblings retreated into the safety of the cave.

"Justice," Nightingale said, "I am afraid."

"As am I," replied her brother, her king. "As am I."

Dark Justice Prologue

He couldn't breathe. The man's lungs dry heaved on the hot, stale air that resided in his mouth. He tried to scream, but his words came muffled to his ears.

There was tape around his mouth.

But not his nose.

Slowly, he took scared breaths through his nostrils. His lungs started to calm down, the heat dissipating as oxygen did its work.

Only then did he open his eyes.

Two other eyes were looking back at his. Pale, grey, dead eyes.

Barnes wanted to rip them out of their sockets. He writhed against the tape that bound his wrists tight behind his back and immobilised his knees and ankles.

"You can't break free," came the voice of his captor. "You're trussed tighter than a prize heifer at a rodeo." The man rose from his crouched position and walked out of Barnes' field of vision. Barnes struggled to manoeuvre himself around on the bare wooden floor to follow the stranger. As he did, something else came into view.

The girl.

"She was innocent." Was that an accent? American? "Poor girl. What did you promise her? Riches? Jewellery? Perhaps it was fame? I doubt it was power." A boot connected with Barnes' chest and pinned him writhing to the floor. "Your type would *never* relinquish power. You thirst for it in all its forms. You suck dry those who possess it like a hungry leech in a stagnant pond. Once you latch onto the power you drink and drink, never full, always hungry for more. When your food supply dries up and dies, you just drop off and float away to your next meal ticket." The tall man bent over the dead girl and ran a finger along her cold flesh. Slowly, he sniffed the digit before running it over in his tongue. "Opiates." The word was low and mournful. "They ruined people in my childhood and yet still they flourish. I'm guessing you were cutting corners, mixing it up with something cheap.

"Something deadly."

In the half light of the shadowy room, the stranger's pale eyes seemed to dance like small fires as he bent low towards his captive. "You have no idea just how worthless you are, little parasite. You swim from host to host, sucking away, happy with your lot, completely unaware of what is going on right under your nose. You see the wars on your television and just treat them like a game show. You hear of catastrophes around the world and think that they have nothing to do with you.

"You have no idea that the end is coming.

"But you can be of use. Yes, you can. You see, I have a purpose, a mission. Others will come after me but they need someone to pave the way for them, flatten the trail so that they can ride all the steadier.

"The world needs to know that my kind exist. It needs to be prepared, and informed that we watch them, protect them." He leant in so close that Barnes could see each of his teeth clearly.

All too clearly.

"And you, my little leech, will bleed so very well."

The duct tape muted the screams that followed.

Nightingale
&
Dave

Nightingale

Nightingale closed her eyes and inhaled deeply of the pungent aroma. It permeated a large, open plan room that was full to the rafters with busy people. The smell that reached her olfactory senses was as old as time; one of warm sweat saturated with the hormones of excitement and anticipation. She smiled. It was a scent that instantly brought her pleasure. A very *human* scent.

"They stink," her companion grumbled. "Do none of them know how to wash?"

The petite brunette opened her eyes and smiled up at her friend. "Don't be such a misery, Marcus. You make it sound like a new phenomenon - the great unwashed." She raised her slim fingers in quotation marks around the last two words. "They are just having fun, as should we."

The tall, greying man harrumphed under his breath in disagreement. "We have responsibilities," he grumbled. "You especially."

The woman smiled quietly to herself, amused by his brusqueness. He was so stuffy for one so young. In her day, the streets had been drenched in this smell. There had been no Calvin Klein, no Chanel, no Lynx effect. Just good old honest sweat with the occasional whiff of lavender should a noble walk past.

She sighed slightly. Yes, many years ago.

She caught herself running a hand up her neck to her new, fashionably short hairstyle. Smells weren't the only things that had altered over the years. Gone were lacy bonnets and demurely covered heads. Now, the sky was the limit with all manner of cuts and colours. The room around them was a testament to that with all sorts of punky styles and bright primary colours.

Hair wasn't the only thing that had shortened in length for women. When had it become acceptable for a room to become so full of legs? There were stripy ones, netted ones, bare ones, painted ones... Again she smiled quietly to herself. She just knew what would be going through Marcus' mind at this moment — thoughts of puritanical horror.

She actually let out a chuckle.

"Nightingale?"

"Nothing," she smiled.

Marcus' grey eyebrows knitted together. "You seem distracted."

Nightingale's eyes scanned the room and she drew in another long breath. "It's okay. There's none in here. You need to relax, enjoy yourself a bit more. You will have a long, tedious existence if you spend it all uptight."

"Is that an order?"

The woman cocked her head to one side and raised an eyebrow. "Does it need to be?"

Marcus was about to reply when a youth wandered up to them and said, "Whoa, guys! Love the outfits!"

Nightingale raised a single eyebrow at the twenty-something clad in what appeared to be a number of old potato sacks stitched together to make a rough tunic which was, in turn, covered by an improvised green cloak fashioned from a blanket. He wore by his side a small plastic sword and he apparently had an aversion to shoes. "Why, thank you," she smiled politely, unaware that Marcus and she had actually come in costume.

"No worries," beamed the ad hoc whatever-he-was. "Your Alex from Being Human is almost perfect. And as for Vincent Price there... Well..." He clapped his hands together and beamed from ear to ear.

Nightingale dipped her head slightly trying not to burst into fits of giggles as she felt Marcus fuming silently by her side. The youth did have a point. There he was, dressed in his impeccably smart suit with a freshly pressed shirt and sporting a silk cravat. Give him slightly wilder hair and a manic stare... It would be quite appropriate all things considered. She gave a demur smile and gently steered Marcus aware before he suffered an apoplexy. "Come now, Vincent dear," she whispered.

"Don't you dare!" he blustered. "I look nothing like the man. Nothing at all."

"If you say so."

Marcus slowly shook his head as his eyes surveyed the room. "What are we doing here?"

"You know what we're doing here."

"Yes, yes. Scorpion had a *vision*." The word dripped with sarcasm. "But why on earth did she have to have one of a fruitcake party?"

Nightingale turned and placed her hands squarely on her hips. Marcus took a small step backwards. "Oh, come on. That's uncalled for," she snapped. "It's just a sci-fi and fantasy convention. They're all harmless and having a great time." She smiled as what looked like a walking carpet shambled past them uttering noises akin to water trying to find its way through a blocked drain. "I think it's kind of fun."

"We're not supposed to be having fun," the male grumbled. "We're supposed to be looking for *him*."

"Well, standing around bickering won't find anybody. I'm going to mingle." With that Nightingale turned on her heel and headed off towards the bar leaving a distraught Marcus stranded on his own like a banker in a children's nursery at messy time.

Nightingale had never been much of an alcohol drinker when she had been younger. This had been for two reasons. First, her employers had frowned upon staff being anything less than sober as a high court judge. The slightest whiff of booze on their breath and they would have been out on their ear. Secondly, there had been very little variety to choose from. There was either the brown swill served in ale houses which tasted of decomposing bread and made hair grow in the most unsightly places, or there were the volatile spirits that crazed alchemists distilled in copper pans in a darkened back room. She had known many an inn go up in flames when the landlord had been trying to perfect another refreshing tonic. So it was that she stood and stared in complete bewilderment at the cornucopia of beverages that adorned the bar in front of her.

"Why do people need a thousand and one ways to destroy their brain cells?" she muttered quietly to herself.

"Probably because they see it as their right."

Nightingale jumped slightly. She had been so engrossed in studying the vast array of optics that she had not noticed the man standing next to her. She mentally chastised herself. She had to be more careful. Slips like that led to disaster. "What do you mean by that?" The question revealed none of the self-admonishment that she was feeling.

The man was slightly taller than average, but not as tall as Marcus. His dark brown hair was cut into a sharp, neat style and he was dressed casually in jeans and a sweatshirt. Altogether Nightingale found him rather appealing. "People see everything as their right these days," he shrugged. "They want the right to get fat. They want the right to talk to others as if they are inferior. They want the right to spend their lives watching trashy television. It makes sense that they want the right to abuse their bodies in as many ways as possible."

"Don't you think that's a rather cynical view of the world?" Nightingale frowned. "Not everyone's like that."

"True, not everyone. Just all those who seem to think that the world is their oyster and treat it as something to rip open so they can extract a nice, shiny pearl." He nodded to the suspended bottles of alcohol. "So what'll be your poison then?"

Nightingale cocked her head slightly to one side, allowing herself a small smile and a flirty twinkle. "Are you buying me a drink?"

The man nodded.

"Well, what would you recommend?"

He appeared to give the matter some thought, then replied, "If we were somewhere that actually knew how to mix something half decent I would say that you'd be a Martini girl. Gin and vermouth with a splash of lemon oil accompanied by an olive. Perfection. However, as their idea of a classy cocktail here is Bacardi and Coke served with a bag of pork scratchings, I'd suggest just sticking to a nice, dry white wine."

Nightingale chuckled. "Sounds good to me."

He caught the attention of one of the many harassed bar staff and ordered two drinks: the wine for Nightingale and a straight vodka on ice for himself. "Cheers," he saluted after paying and clinked his glass against Nightingale's. "So tell me then, what are you doing here?"

"I'm here for the convention," Nightingale lied smoothly as she sipped her drink. It really did taste rather nice.

The stranger shook his head. "No you're not. Look around you. All these guys are here for the convention. They're absorbed in it, engrossed in their fantasy worlds. Whereas you... You are outside of that little glass fish bowl looking in."

Nightingale looked at her drinking companion over the rim of her wineglass. His dark eyes were fixed on her. At that moment she was the sole attention of his world. Could he be..? "I'm looking for someone," she volunteered. "A man."

A cruel smirk crept onto the stranger's mouth and she knew that she had been mistaken. This was not him. There was just going to be a line. Something like, "Well, I guess you've found him, sweetheart," or, "Think I'll be man enough for you?"

What he *actually* said chilled her to the bone.

"You'll never find him, *vampire*."

The word hissed into her ears like a curse and she sat silent, shocked.

The stranger leant forward, the smell of alcohol on his breath. "You will fail. You will *all* fail. The Divergence is coming and we are everywhere. The dragon shall rise and this world will be his."

Two things struck Nightingale simultaneously. The first was one word that leapt into her head.

Construct.

The second was a sharp knife that plunged into her stomach.

Instinct took over. She had been a fool and let her guard down. First, it had walked right up next to her without her realisation, then it had actually sat and flirted with her without her getting so much as a whiff of its scent. Now she had to start thinking like the professional killer that she was. Quickly she turned towards the bar and, covering the blade from sight, pulled it out of her gut in one swift move. She stashed it inside her leather jacket and turned to see her quarry sprinting out of the bar. She pressed her fingers tight against the wound as the skin started to heal beneath her clothes.

Nightingale took off in pursuit, careful not to allow her supernatural speed take over and cause a commotion. She had to remain, for all onlookers at least, outwardly human. As she ran across the room, she felt Marcus fall in time with her.

"What happened?"

"Construct," she cursed. "Male, slightly shorter than you, brown hair. I'm guessing he's making for his car." Her voice was strained.

"You sound hurt."

"The bastard stabbed me. I'll heal."

The two vampires hurried out into the cool night air and breathed deeply. There was the creature's scent, clear as a day that neither of them could walk in. How had she missed it before? Had she been so preoccupied with Scorpion's vision? Obviously she had.

She had to make amends. The construct could not be allowed to escape.

There was the roar of a car engine turning over and a red estate flew past them. In an instant Marcus was clinging on to the roof of the car as it swayed across the parking lot, narrowly missing another vehicle that was parked by a tree. Nightingale chased after them, her legs moving in a blur. She too managed to lay a hand on the car as it growled up the incline to the road but then she felt her grip thrown off along with Marcus as the car spun round a corner.

They quickly recovered themselves in time to see a sight that stopped them both dead in their tracks. As the construct pushed his foot to the floor someone stepped out into the road in front of him. The car did not even slow down. It ploughed into the unfortunate bystander and shot off towards the motorway.

Nightingale sprang up in the air and descended next to the casualty. He was lying in a heap at the side of the road. His arms were at peculiar angles and his right leg had an extra joint.

There was also blood. Lots of it.

"Oh no," Nightingale gasped as she knelt by the broken body.

"Nightingale!"

She bent over and stroked a finger down the man's cheek. He was in one of the costumes that she had seen people wearing in the convention: a blue shirt, dark hair and pointy plastic ears.

"Nightingale! Quick. He's getting away."

"It's my fault," she whispered. "If I hadn't let my guard down..." She paused as she felt a flutter in the man's neck. "He's still alive! Marcus, he's still alive!" With as much care as she could manage she rolled the bleeding man onto his back. He lay there cradled in her arms, blood flowering on his chest. "Oh no," she whispered again.

"We have to go," Marcus urged, pacing impatiently behind her on the footpath. "We can still catch it."

The man gave an almost imperceptible groan as his eyes flickered open. He gazed up at Nightingale through rivulets of his own blood and performed the unbelievable.

He smiled.

"We can't just leave him here." Nightingale pressed her fingers against his neck again. "His pulse is very weak."

"We have to. We have a job to do."

You will finally find your child. The words sang in Nightingale's head as she cradled the dying man. "Tigress was insistent about Scorp's vision. She said I would find my child. That's why we came here, not to chase some walking lump of clay." Gently, she brushed the man's hair away from his wet face. "I came here to find *you*," she whispered so quietly that only another vampire could hear it.

"That's ridiculous!" Marcus hissed, "We have to go. Others will be here soon. It's getting late and people will be making their way home."

Nightingale shook her head. "I'm not leaving him. He's near death. I have to save him." Her voice was icily cold.

"So now, after all these years, you decide to generate a child? Here at the side of a road. How romantic!" he harrumphed.

"Stop being so stuck up and just keep watch," Nightingale ordered, then to the man in her arms she soothed, "Relax, my child. Soon you will feel no pain," and she sank her sharp teeth into his neck to drain him dry. It took very little time as the majority of his blood was already shed on the footpath. The thick, red liquid was sweet as it coursed down her oesophagus into her stomach. She felt it seep its way into her gut and circulate into her own veins. When she was sure that it was integrated into her own systems she bit into her wrist and offered the wound up to his mouth for him to drink. At first, the recipient just lay still and the blood could only drip into his slack mouth, but after a moment his jaw began to move rhythmically and the vampire felt suction against her skin as the blood started to spurt. As Nightingale watched her child feed, she saw his wounds close up and his broken limbs straighten out.

Just then, there was the sound of a car ignition from the parking lot. "Nightingale! We have to go now!" Marcus placed a hand on her shoulder and gently pulled.

She looked down at her child despairingly. "He's not finished."

"*We'll* be finished if people find us here."

The new mother looked up frantically and saw attendees of the convention piling out of the hotel. With resignation, she nodded and bent close to her newborn's ear. "Listen to me." Her voice was no more than the wind blowing in the air, but she knew that his new accentuated hearing could pick out every word. "I have to go now but I *will* find you. If you remember anything of this, then make sure it is what I am about to tell you." She steeled herself and repeated the three things that every Child of Cain was told at its creation: "Find the Eternals. Protect the Twins. Await the Divergence." Then, as carefully as a mother lies her baby in a cot, she lowered his head to the floor.

Nightingale stood, nodded at Marcus and the two of them vanished into the night as bloody tears streaked down her porcelain face. She had a child now. She would find him again because that was her responsibility. Then, when she had found him, she would train him, guide him in the ways of their kind and watch him flourish, because that was what mothers did.

First Hunt - Now

The black four by four drew to a halt on the sparsely gravelled path. A pair of legs swung out from a rear door into the cool, moonlit night. Their owner drew in a deep refreshing breath of highland air and smiled to himself. It was a curious sensation as he performed it just for pleasure not for the act of respiration.

He had no need for that now.

He was, for all intents and purposes, dead.

"You okay?"

Dave Nichols, former proprietor of a small comic book shop in a city in the North West of England, turned to the woman (if you could call her that) who had taken his mortal life. "Never been better," he smiled. "Never been better."

Nightingale closed the passenger's door with a solid click and made her way round to her newly born offspring. She took his hand in hers and smiled up into his eyes. "Good. I'm glad."

"Everything feels so different," the newborn whispered into the night. "I know that's cliché but..."

"That's okay. I was totally the same. There's so much for you to learn. That's why we've come here."

There was a solid clunk as the driver's door shut. "So hadn't we better get on with it then?" came a clipped, masculine voice. "We only have a few hours until sunrise."

"Patience, Marcus." Nightingale turned to her long-standing companion. "We'll go and settle ourselves down in the cabin. We'll be perfectly safe in there when the sun comes up." With that, she led her companion and her child up the gravel path towards the old cabin that stood overlooking the sea from the cliffside. After just a few steps, she and the older of the two males stopped dead in their tracks.

"What is it?" Dave asked.

Nightingale flicked a sidewards glance to Marcus and he was suddenly a blur of colour as he streaked up the rest of the path to the cabin and in through the door.

"Nightingale..."

She held a hand up to silence her child as her sharp eyes scanned the ground between them and the cabin. A few seconds later, Marcus opened the door again and walked at a more sedate pace back towards the car. "It's all clear," he said.

Nightingale frowned. "But they've definitely been here." It was a statement, not a question.

Marcus nodded slowly. "There's something else, too."

Nightingale cocked her head to one side in a question but her progeny cut in before Marcus could answer. "Who? Who's been here?"

The young mother looked her child straight in the eye. "Constructs."

Dave looked on feeling somewhat helpless as the other two vampires circled the immediate area around the cabin. Every now and then, one or both of them would stand still, scent the air then crouch to examine the rough ground. He had no idea what was going on. It was obviously something of importance and danger, but as to its exact nature...

So he stood propped against the four by four and waited until the others had completed their recce before making their way back to him. "What's going on?" he asked.

"This is supposed to be a safe house," Nightingale explained. "We often bring new-borns here to help them through their initial transition and to train them. It is known to no one outside of our community."

"And yet constructs have been here," Marcus growled, his eyes flitting from spot to spot as if seeing things that were not there, "and there's been fighting."

Dave ran his fingers through his sandy-coloured hair. "Okay. So I'm guessing this is bad?"

Nightingale nodded. "Very."

"And there's more." Marcus began pointing to various spots around the cabin. "There's been some sort of battle here. There is dried blood on the ground and bullet cases. There was a firefight."

Dave frowned. "Bullets? So they weren't after a vampire then?"

Nightingale smiled. "Good logic. The blood is neither construct nor vampire. Come and see this." She led her child over to the edge of the cliff. "See here where the stone has crumbled? There are splatter patterns around the damaged stone. Bend down close and smell it."

Dave did as instructed. He knelt on one knee and lowered his nose to the ground. He caught a symphony of fragrances: grass, soil, sea, rock and... and... He gasped as the sweetest aroma he had ever smelled hit his brain. "Wow! What is that? I feel like I'm smelling a rainbow!"

Marcus turned to Nightingale and lifted a sardonic eyebrow. Nightingale smiled softly. "We don't know. It's definitely not construct. You remember what that tasted like?"

Dave nodded, recalling a few nights ago back in Lancaster when his new instincts had taken over and he had attacked a woman who, at the time, he had not consciously known to be a construct. "It was dark, artificial – as if someone had made something to appear like human blood but had not quite got it right. There was also that grainy aftertaste."

"Correct." Nightingale crouched down next to him. "Quite unlike your friend's blood."

Dave shuddered at that thought. He had been forced to drink the blood of Sam Spallucci, the man who had been taking care of him. If he had not done so, he would have remained incomplete. "His blood was so... alive."

"Exactly. Sam is a living creature. Constructs are just what their name suggests. They have been made to look like humans. This, however," she traced a finger along the dark stain on the rocks, "is something completely different. Someone very special was here."

Dave straightened up and ran his fingers through his mop of hair. "This is so confusing. There's so much to learn. Tell me more. Tell me about the constructs."

"They are soulless demons." Marcus' deep voice cut across the still night. "They have no conscience or ounce of goodness in them. They are creations, simulacra intended to infiltrate humanity and sit there, waiting."

"Waiting? What for?"

Nightingale stood and idly brushed some dirt off her trousers. "We're not entirely sure. Part of the problem is that most of them do not know what they are. They are sleeper agents of some sort, programmed to wake at a specific moment or cue. They can spend years thinking they are human.

They may have mundane, day-to-day jobs or they may have positions of power. Wherever they are we have to track them down and kill them."

"Why?"

Nightingale answered with deep sadness. "Because if we don't, then they will eradicate our kind. As soon as they awaken then their true nature becomes manifest, and they will hunt down the nearest Child of Cain and slaughter him or her no matter what the consequence. We have lost many to them."

The three vampires started to walk towards the cabin as the youngster mulled this over.

"So, if they are sleepers, then who programmed them?"

"Kanor." The one word from Marcus' lips was spat like a curse. "Until you had your vision, we had no name for him, but now we know our enemy."

Dave stopped and stared down at his feet. "And I will die in his presence."

He felt a cool hand brush his cheek. "We cannot change our future, my child, but we can do what we must for that which we hold to be of utmost importance."

He lifted his eyes and looked into Nightingale's sad orbs. "Find the Eternals. Protect the Twins. Await the Divergence."

Nightingale nodded. "That's right. That is what the very first of our kind was instructed to do, and we must follow his example."

They resumed their walk to the cabin. "By *our very first*, do you mean Cain?"

Marcus opened the old wooden door and they entered the shack. It was dark and smelt musty. There were, however, obvious signs that it had been recently inhabited: a dead fire in the hearth, blankets on the small bed and food left discarded on the table. The older of the two male vampires picked up the stale bread and sniffed it with disgust. "Cain was visited by a stranger just after he slew his brother, Abel. He was full to the brim with remorse and regret at his rash action. The stranger gave him a chance for redemption. He turned him into a vampire and told him to go out and spread his kind amongst the human world with those three instructions. So that is what we have done since the dawn of civilisation." He tossed the bread with precision into a bucket that sat next to the fire. A small cloud of ashes plumed up in its wake.

"So," Dave asked as he settled into a creaking wooden chair that felt in danger of imminent collapse, "who was the stranger?"

Nightingale perched in front of him on the table and smiled. "He was an angel. We have angelic blood coursing through our veins."

It was starting to be a night of revelations: creatures fashioned and sent by some big bad to wipe out vampires; the father of all vampires was an angel. If he had been a smoker, then Dave would have been puffing his way through a pack of twenty.

"Are there any more little secrets you'd like to tell me about?"

His mother smiled lovingly at him. "Oh, there are plenty, my child, but right now we have a more pressing matter." She rose and made her way over to a grubby window. Closing her eyes, she inhaled deeply before turning to her companion. "Two?" she asked.

"That was my count," Marcus agreed. "Over in the woods. I would imagine they have seen us and are waiting to see where we go so that they can follow us."

Nightingale nodded. "Very well." Turning to Dave, she grinned. "Well, it appears tonight you shall have your first practical lesson.

"You're going to learn how to hunt."

A short while later, Dave was creeping through the undergrowth of a nearby copse with Nightingale at his side. He was trying his best to move stealthily but, to his hypersensitive hearing, every step sounded like a thunderclap and every broken stick a gunshot. "Surely they'll hear us?" he asked in a voice that sounded to him like a tornado ripping through a densely populated city.

Nightingale slowly shook her head, not for once taking her eyes off the shadows that danced between the trees in the moonlight. "We are superior in every way. We move faster and with greater stealth. We have heightened senses. They are no different to humans except for their physical makeup. They will not hear us unless we make a drastic mistake."

"Physical makeup?"

"Constructs are not creatures of flesh and blood," the older vampire explained. "They are made from a clay-like substance that allows them to resemble humans and blend into society. Be careful, though. They are killers and can adapt their form accordingly."

Dave ran his fingers through his hair again. He felt less than reassured. "So whereabouts is Marcus now?"

"Close your eyes and inhale slowly. See what your senses tell you."

The young vampire did as he was instructed. He lightly closed his eyelids and drew a long, deep breath in through his nose. There were the fresh green leaves, the grass, the soil. Those scents were all-pervading as if he was enveloped in a blanket woven by Mother Nature herself. Then there was an acrid tang that reminded him of cities. Diesel? Yes, it was the car in which they had driven to this place. Curiously, he could pinpoint it way back behind them, which told him that the cabin lay a small distance to their rear. He concentrated on what was passing over the cells in his nose and picked up two more distinct smells. One was crisp and clean, fresh with the scent of expensive cologne. That was Marcus. He let his brain play with the strength and intensity that it recognised as the norm for when the older vampire was standing in his presence and that, along with his skin feeling the slight breeze of the night, gave him an answer. He was just about to say that their companion was in the region of fifty metres away when the second scent muscled its way into his senses.

Dave grunted with revulsion. It was a scent that was wrong. It smelt human but had an earthy undercurrent that told of dark, dank places next to foetid swamps. He almost gagged as he snapped his eyes open and rubbed his mouth on the back of his hand.

Nightingale was looking straight at him. "Good. You smelt them, didn't you?"

"Yes, they are very close. Marcus is a bit further away."

"He will come at them from the other side as planned," she explained. "Lead on. Take me to them." She gestured with her arm deeper into the woods.

As the two vampires walked slowly through the dense undergrowth, a stray thought crossed Dave's mind. "Nightingale?"

"Yes, my child."

"Do we have a leader? Some sort of King Vampire?"

He expected an amused chuckle, but instead there was a sorrowful sigh. "That is an awkward question to answer at the moment."

"Why?"

"Well," Nightingale paused as she obviously sought out the simplest explanation, "we do have a structure for leadership. To simplify it somewhat, our leader has always been the oldest vampire in the bloodline closest to the original source. So, in the beginning it would have been Cain. Cain then had children. When he died, his oldest took on the role of leader. When *he* died then his child took over and so on. If the vampire died without leaving an heir then their sibling would become king or queen. It is very similar to human monarchy."

"Okay, so who is in charge now, then?"

Nightingale stopped and leaned against a tree. "The situation is somewhat *complex*."

Dave frowned. "How?"

"The head of the line at the moment never wanted to be king. To make it worse, he..." She momentarily examined the earth at her feet before looking back up. "He suffered a great loss that broke his mind. He is not stable."

"So you have no leader at the moment?"

"We have a *regent*."

"And who is that?"

Silence hung between them in the woods until Nightingale volunteered, "That would be me. And now we are going to change the subject. We have work to do."

Dave gave a quick nod. He guessed it was best not to annoy the new boss. "So what's the plan?"

"You go in there quickly and you kill them both."

Dave felt his stomach clench with sudden apprehension. "Me?" he hissed in the dark.

There was no reply. He turned to where Nightingale had been standing and saw empty woods. He was on his own.

Nightingale looked down from the canopy. She could easily make out her child down below. He was frantically turning this way and that in blind panic, all recent lessons apparently forgotten, as he tried to locate her. Not once did he look up. She smiled softly. This would be fun to watch. As light as her namesake she skipped from branch to branch hardly causing a stir. The reddening leaves of autumn did not rustle and within a few seconds she was nestled at the top of a large tree by a clearing.

There they were.

She inhaled slowly. The air reeked of them: their foulness, their wrongness. She swallowed hungrily as she yearned to leap down and dispatch them, drain them of their life force, but that was not to be tonight. Not unless something went drastically wrong.

Tonight belonged to her offspring, just as the night of her first hunt had belonged to her so many years ago. Her brow creased with amusement. Who was she kidding? She was under two hundred years old, a mere child in vampire years. There were others out there who were in their thousands; ones who had seen ancient empires rise and fall.

Yet she was their superior. She was their ruler through right of birth. This was not a path she desired, but such was her fate. It had fallen in her lap and she had to deal with it, just as, one day, she would have to deal with her older brother.

However, that was a thought for another time. Right now, she had to watch and wait.

"Okay, okay," Dave muttered under his breath, "I can do this. I've done it before without even thinking. It can't be that hard, can it?" He thought back to the night in Lancaster. Instinct had taken over automatically. He had sensed the construct and just reacted. His muscles had responded without any prompting and he had zeroed in on her, grasping her tight and plunging his teeth in.

Rhythmically, he rocked back on the balls of his feet, concentrating on the two presences in the clearing ahead. He focussed all his senses on them and felt his body prepare for the charge. His stomach growled in hunger. That was good. That was good. He was ready. Yes, he was.

He swung his arms back and forth by his sides just as he used to in gym class when he was preparing to sprint down the running track. Back and forth they swung, long pendulums building up potential power ready to propel him after his prey.

He closed his eyes, breathed deep, placed a foot forward ready to run and...

Came to a sudden stop after one foot fall.

What was he doing?

This was insane!

They had not done anything to him. How could he take their lives? He had been repulsed after his attack on the girl in the Sugar House. It had made him physically sick. When he had found her corpse outside, exsanguinated and dumped, it had screamed against all his moral values.

It had been wrong.

He ran his fingers through his sandy hair in frustration. Oh, this was not good. What was he to do?

He had an idea. He would go and watch them first, creep up to the edge of the clearing and spy on them. Surely if they were evil incarnate then he would be able to see so and then he would attack.

Yes. That was what he would do. That was a plan.

With a large helping of stealth and a good dose of trepidation, Dave carefully picked his way to the edge of the clearing. Gradually, he began to make out darkness rather than trees as he approached the edge of the wooded area. His ears picked out two voices as his prey talked to each other. He listened in. It was hardly the machinations of evil geniuses. They were discussing television. One was berating the judges of Strictly Come Dancing for letting some overweight TV chef take part even though, in the speaker's honest opinion, he was completely talentless. His companion berated him and told him not to be so heartless. He told him that it was only a television show, not the end of the world. They then went on to discuss the X Factor and Simon Cowell.

Dave frowned. They could not be evil creatures, surely? Did Nightingale have it wrong? Was she mistaken? Had his own senses deceived him earlier? There was only one way to find out.

He stepped out into the clearing.

"Hello there!" he called out.

What on Earth was he doing? Nightingale almost broke the branch of the tree as her grip increased exponentially at her sudden anxiety. Her eyes must surely be deceiving her. Dave was actually walking over to the constructs and talking to them.

Actually talking to them!

She looked over to the other side of the clearing. She could just make out the broken outline of Marcus partially obscured by undergrowth. He had her child covered, but all the same, this was going horribly wrong.

What was he thinking? Part of her was screaming that she ought to jump down and intervene, slay the creatures where they stood, but that would defeat the object of the exercise. This was Dave's night. She had to leave him be.

And other vampires wondered why she had taken so long to decide to become a mother...

The two men turned and faced Dave as he stepped out of the tree line. He saw looks of worry pass between their confused faces.

Okay, he could do this. "No need to panic. I was just passing by and overheard you."

One of the strangers turned towards him. "In a forest? In the middle of the night?"

Dave winced. Yes, it did sound odd now he thought about it. "I... like night walks," he smiled amiably. "They're so refreshing."

Both of the strangers were now standing up in the middle of the clearing, providing him with a perfect view of them. One was in his forties, fairly stout with grey hair and the other was a few years younger, slim and blonde. Both of them had a backpack on the ground at their feet. They looked for all intents and purposes like a couple of walkers. Certainly not like homicidal maniacs.

If anyone filled that role right now, it was the crazy guy who had just walked out of the woods. Dave sighed. This was not going to plan. "Listen, to be honest, I'm kind of lost. I think I took the wrong path awhile back. Have you guys got a map?"

The younger one looked to the older who raised an eyebrow and shrugged. "Sure," said blondie. "It's in my pack. Come over here and I'll dig it out for you." He bent over and started to unfasten his bag.

Dave walked over to the two men and presented his friendliest smile. "Well, this is very kind of you." As he turned to watch the younger man rummage in his bag, he heard a noise that sounded like mud sliding off a wellington boot. His instincts screamed and he swivelled to see the older man bearing down on him. His attacker's hand had transformed into a long, dark stake. It was being thrust towards his chest when there was a blur and suddenly the man's head was missing. The decapitated body carried forward with its momentum pushing it on and toppled over at Dave's feet. He saw Marcus coming to a stop a couple of metres away with the man's head in his hands.

The young vampire felt a change in the air around him and, without thinking, leapt at the blonde man who was now charging towards Marcus. Dave flew through the air and clung onto his target's back, gripping his prey's right hand as it slipped and slid into a long, hard weapon akin to that of his late companion's. The construct discharged a rough grunt as it was manhandled to the floor. Rage and hunger welled up inside the hunter who drew his head back, exposing his sharp teeth, before plunging them down into his victim's neck.

The vampire drank heavily, imbibing furiously on the thick liquid that passed for the creature's blood. As he drank, he felt the writhing and wriggling of his prey lessen and its physical form weakened under his weight. He gripped the creature tight in his grasp and, as its skin desiccated, he felt its stake-hand snap off between his tightly clasping fingers.

Then there was nothing. The husk of a body could give him no more.

It was empty and Dave's immediate hunger had been sated.

He pushed off from the corpse and cried into the still night air as fire rocketed around his veins and capillaries. Kneeling in the grass, he panted heavily as his dead heart pumped invigorated lifeblood around his body. He realised that his eyes were closed and when he opened them he saw Marcus draining the decapitated remains of the other construct. He had sunk his teeth deep into one of its wrists and was sucking every drop of remnant life from its withering form.

A soft footstep drew Dave's heightened attention and he felt a familiar hand caress his hair. He leaned into his mother's touch.

"Come, my child," soothed Nightingale's soft voice. "The night is late, and we have much to do."

Visions and Prophecies

"Well, this isn't exactly what I was expecting."

Nightingale tried her best to suppress a smile as she watched her offspring gaze around the small public house in a somewhat bemused fashion. It was on the corner of a pedestrian precinct in Sale, a commuter belt for Manchester. Not exactly what Dave had thought would be *vampire central*. "Really?" she asked. "Why might that be?"

"Is that a whippet sat next to the guy at the bar?"

"Perhaps it's a specially trained *scout* whippet?" She was finding it next to impossible to stop a wicked chuckle breaking up her words, but she was just about managing it.

"You have that sort of thing?" Dave's voice was a mixture of confusion and awe.

There was a despairing sigh from behind them and Marcus strode through the overly mundane room to a discreet door in a quiet corner. "She's playing with you," he explained. "We need to go through here."

Nightingale finally dissolved.

"Oh…" was all that her offspring could manage before hurrying through the door that his mother's companion now held open whilst sporting a withering look of annoyance.

"Spoilsport," the diminutive vampire whispered to her smartly dressed companion. "I was only having fun."

Marcus looked down at his regent. "That's not what we are here for though, is it?"

Nightingale rolled her eyes and followed her child through the small door to the other world.

"Now *this* is more like it." Dave's eyes wandered round the back room. There was a long, highly polished bar that sported a number of gleaming pumps with a multitude of optics hanging behind on the wall. A white-haired, attractive woman winked at him as she methodically polished glasses. Some patrons were sat at the bar; a number were talking quietly in booths. Two, a pair of women — one sporting short cut red hair, the other long, flowing blonde locks — were dancing maniacally on a small dance floor by the juke box to something poppy and unmistakably eighties by *Wham!* The redhead looked over her partner's shoulder and caught sight of the three newcomers.

"Nightingale!" she shouted.

"Hey, Tigress," Nightingale called back. "How's things?"

The redhead broke off from her frenetic gyrating and walked over with the blonde. Dave glanced down and noticed that they were holding hands. "Oh, you know. Same old, same old." Her green eyes turned to Dave. "So you found him them?"

Nightingale nodded.

"Told ya! Scorp's always right. Aren't ya, babe?"

The pretty blonde nodded mutely.

"So, newbie? What's your name?"

"Oh, it's Dave. Dave Nichols," Dave managed.

Tigress raised a perfectly arched eyebrow. "Seriously? You're going with *Dave*?" Then, to Nightingale, "Where'd you find this guy?"

"At a comic convention."

Her brow still raised, Tigress eyed Dave up and down as if appraising a cheap *Primark* dress that had inexplicably found its way onto a mannequin in *Harrods*. "Well," she finally said, "At least he's not dressed like Spock."

Dave blushed.

Marcus sighed.

Nightingale sniggered.

Tigress' jaw dropped. "No way! She made you a vamp when you were wearing pointy ears?" Her laughter filled the bar. Eventually, when she had brought herself under control, she gripped her focus of fun by the hand. "Welcome to Vixen's Den. That's Vix over there," she pointed to the woman behind the bar who was watching them intently and pulled Dave close, before whispering in his ear, "Just watch your pants. Maneater. Know what I mean?" Then back at normal volume, "I, as you must be aware by now, am Tigress, and this," she grinned, dragging her mute partner closer, "Is Scorpion." The blonde smiled bashfully. "She don't say much, well she don't say anything to anyone apart from me, but she's amazing."

Dave watched Tigress' green eyes fix on her other half and the flow of love from the brash redhead to the silent blonde was unmistakable.

"I believe that I sort of owe you my life," Dave said to the quiet vampire. "If you hadn't sent Nightingale after me…" His voice trailed off. "Thank you." He stuck out his hand.

Scorpion shrugged an *it's nothing* and took the proffered hand of friendship.

Their palms connected then…

…everything changed.

The first thing that hit Dave was the heat — the blinding, scorching heat.

The second was the sun.

He cried out in fear and dived for cover. He was in a small street next to a large stone building and threw himself behind some abandoned boxes and pitchers. It was no good, though. The sun still beat down on him and its insatiable heat licked every millimetre of his porcelain skin.

However, he did not burn.

There was no scorching of skin, no frying of flesh, no other combustible alliteration.

What he did feel was a hand slip into his. A slender hand, soft and feminine. He looked up at its owner and Scorpion smiled down at him. She motioned with her head and he followed her down the street of a city that was quite obviously situated somewhere hotter than the Manchester that they had apparently left behind. As well as the warm sun, there was the crunch of sand on the paving stones and a hint of the sea in the air. It was also somewhere very old. People walked down the street oblivious to the two vampires. There was no modern technology. In fact, there was no technology that seemed to have seen the light of day for over two thousand years. The citizens wore toga-like robes. Mules pulled carts. A small group of soldiers ran past carrying small shields and bronze-tipped lances.

"Where are we?" Dave asked.

Scorpion squeezed his hand and increased her pace, following after the soldiers. Dave accompanied her. They twisted through the rabbit warren of streets until they emerged at a large square by the massive gates of the city wall. Dave could not help but gape in amazement at the enormous portico that towered higher than many twenty-first century buildings. The walls were truly impenetrable.

Then, when he walked out onto the beach before the city, he knew exactly where he was.

A massive wooden horse stood in front of him.

"Okay," he whispered to his silent companion, "two questions. One, can anyone see us?"

He watched Scorpion study the inhabitants of Troy as they poured out of the city to view the massive equine gift. Not once did they pause to regard the two strangers in their unusual clothing. They just seemed to walk around them as if they were somehow guided around an unseen obstacle.

Scorpion shook her head.

"Right. Well, that's good. So, next question. Why are we here?"

There was no immediate reply, not that he really expected one from the elective mute, however he noticed that she was gazing off into the crowd that was forming in front of the horse. He followed her line of sight and saw what was a small selection of citizens from the higher echelons of society. Their robes were made from lusher material and dyed in rich colours. Two women, in particular, stood out from the crowd. One was clad in a light blue gown and a gold tiara was threaded through her dark, immaculately cut hair. The other, standing next to her, stood out from the rest of the crowd, her hair a cascading waterfall of blonde in complete contrast to the surrounding roiling sea of dark locks. The blonde's lips moved as she turned to look up at the other woman and Dave felt Scorpion's hand involuntarily squeeze his.

"Well, that must be rather weird for you," he whispered.

The taller woman turned and said something to the other Scorpion before raising a hand and tenderly stroking her cheek then bending down and kissing her forehead. Dave afforded *his* Scorpion a quick glance and saw a small bead of blood trickle down her alabaster cheek. Unsure what to say, he snatched his head back to the women in front and studied the darker-haired woman.

She was the definition of beauty. Her glossy hair shone in the daylight and her eyes sparkled like the sea before them. The gown covered her body but was far from modest — it highlighted every curve and hinted at potential carnal pleasures.

This was a woman who was used to being worshipped.

Yet Dave found he could feel nothing for her. There was something about her that told a story of vanity and cruelty. He seriously did not want to be on the receiving end of her anger.

There was a commotion over by the horse where a bearded man was waving his hands and shouting to the staring onlookers. His tongue sounded familiar but not fully understandable. Dave heard glimpses of Latin but the inflection and phraseology did not ring true. However, the message of the man, as he ranted and screamed at the onlookers whilst gesticulating wildly at the horse, was obvious no matter what language you spoke.

"Beware of Greeks bearing gifts," Dave recited.

There was a murmur through the crowd, which seemed to be falling under the sway of the protestor. The man nodded and smiled at their response.

But then there was a commotion behind him. Something in the water.

People started to shout and point as the sea bubbled and rolled up onto the shore. They became nervous and agitated, anticipating some sort of ill. Then there was a rush of water up into the sky like liquid being poured out of a jug, but defying the basic law of gravity that would not be discovered for many, many years. The water spout coalesced and twisted into a serpentine form that spun and thrashed as if it were alive. It barrelled towards the shore and, at its head, a mouth opened.

Everyone screamed.

All except one. The dark-haired woman watched impassively as the sea creature reared its head above the bearded protestor. All she did was wave her fingers in small movements by her side. She twirled them and the serpent twisted, she flicked them and its head swayed from side to side, she pointed them to the floor and it hammered down, its mouth swallowing up the unfortunate man before dragging him away into the ocean.

Then, as everyone else ran around in blind panic or fell to their knees begging forgiveness of the gods, she smiled, placed her arm around her version of Scorpion and turned to walk back towards the city that the next day would be in flames because of her actions. As she climbed up from the beach, she paused momentarily by Dave and *his* Scorpion and frowned. Dave felt his throat dry with fear and Scorpion held very still beside him, then the woman shook her head, took her ward and walked away.

Then…

…everything changed.

They were in a forest. Immediately, their senses pricked.

Fire!

There was the unmistakable stench of something sizeable and wooden burning out of control. An ominous smog of black smoke lazed its way through the dense trees. For a split second, Dave thought he heard Scorpion gasp, then she was gone, darting into the black pall. He cursed, not wanting to be left behind, and followed the quick flashes of her long, blonde hair that cast the occasional waymarker to follow in the gloom.

In a short while, he found her stood behind a tree, peering round at a clearing where a small cottage burned like a warning beacon in the dark. Off to one side, on the tree line, Dave could make out three figures. Two were bent over another, who was lying cradled in their arms. Again, he could not fail to recognise the long blonde hair of another Scorpion. There, with her, was Tigress. He did not recognise the man that lay in their arms.

Gently, he tapped his Scorpion on the shoulder. "You remember this?" he enquired.

The sadness in her face was all the answer that he needed.

The three were talking quietly. Dave tried to listen, but the roar of the blazing house masked their hushed words. Then the man's hand fell from Tigress' face and, for a while, there was no movement as the two vampires sat in silent grief. However, the tender moment of loss was shattered when an unmistakable scream of rage from Tigress cut through the forest. The redheaded vampire rose from the forest floor and rampaged around the clearing, shouting and screaming obscenities into the dark, annihilating anything in the cottage that had not already been devoured by the flames. The other Scorpion just continued to cradle the dead man, rocking silently back and forth.

Dave felt *his* Scorpion take a step forward. He flung his arms around her narrow waist and dragged her back. "No! No! We can't."

There was anger in her blue eyes with a heat comparable to the blazing fire as she frantically struggled to escape his grip.

"I'm sorry, I really am, but we can't interfere. Do you remember you being here? You can't change the past. It has dire consequences. There was this classic episode of *Star Trek*. Joan Collins was in it. Kirk and the others went back in time and... Ow!" He flinched as the struggling Scorpion bit his arm and broke free.

Dave threw himself forward and rugby-tackled his time-travelling companion. Even as she fell heavily to the floor, she still didn't make a sound. He scrambled up her back and pressed his greater weight down on her smaller form. It was like trying to wrestle a cobra. Her lithe body rolled and undulated beneath him as her teeth tried to bite and slash at his face. Eventually, Dave managed to grab the back of her neck and pushed her face into the mud. "I'm sorry, for this," he panted, "I really am, but we cannot interfere with the timeline. We just can't."

Scorpion struggled a small while longer then lay ominously still. Dave tentatively leant forward.

All he could hear were plaintive, childlike sobs.

Then...

...everything changed.

Dave felt a firm shove from underneath him and he rolled over onto his back. Scorpion pulled herself up to a seated position and slowly wiped her face clean. The two of them stayed there, silently watching each other.

Inevitably it was the younger vampire that spoke first. "Why don't you speak?"

Scorpion's eyes flicked away from him and she doodled in the dirt with a finger, before allowing him a nonplussed shrug.

An insolent rise and fall of the shoulders was better than nothing, so Dave decided to pursue the matter. "Back in Troy, you were talking to that woman. You were human then?"

A small nod.

Dave chewed his bottom lip as he recalled the woman's affection to his companion.

"Did you love her?"

Another small nod. This one almost imperceptible.

"Did she hurt you?"

Scorpion's eyes focused on the soil where she was doodling. A tiny drip of blood splattered the dry ground.

"She looked powerful. Who was she?"

Scorpion sent a daggered eye stab to her inquisitor that clearly said, "No more questions," before getting up, dusting herself down and walking off a small distance.

Dave rolled himself to all fours then up to his feet. As he did so, he looked at what the annoyed woman had been doodling in the dust. It looked like an upper case letter T with two swirls wrapped around it. He sighed. This was going nowhere.

Then he heard the unmistakable squeal of tyres and the sickening thud of a body hitting a car bonnet.

He felt chilled when he realised where they were.

They were behind a modern building, a huge concrete monstrosity which Dave recalled was a gym on the outskirts of Lancaster. He jogged quietly to the corner of the complex just in time to see the car that had just hit his former self squealing off into the night. Two figures tore across the car park of the hotel opposite and hovered over his broken body.

He knew this scene.

It was still fresh in his memory.

Nightingale bending over him, carefully tending to him. Marcus urging that they leave.

He saw his mother sink her teeth into her own flesh and offer her blood to him. He heard the noise of others coming out of the comic convention and the vampires were gone. Slowly, unsteadily, his former self staggered to his feet, groaned at the sight of his tattered *Star Trek* uniform and limped off into town.

There was a soft scuff of gravel next to him. Dave turned and saw Scorpion looking on in amusement.

"What?"

She reached up and tickled the top of his ears, giggling silently.

Dave could not help but smile too.

Then…

…everything changed.

Screams.

Screams everywhere.

Screams and the sickening sound of clay transforming shape.

Dave and Scorpion were stood on a plateau above what could only be described as apocalyptic carnage.

"Are those… angels?"

Scorpion nodded.

"They're not doing very well, are they?"

Scorpion shook her head.

It was a massacre. An army of white-clad angels were being quite literally shredded by a horde of constructs. There were ripped wings and feathers being trampled into the bloodied ground and pierced bodies lay strewn across the field.

"What the hell is this?"

Scorpion's hand squeezed his and he looked up to a higher hill where another battle was taking place. Two figures clashed with swords, swiping ferociously again and again in an attempt to strike each other down.

"They really don't like each other do they?"

There was no response from his companion. She was staring intently at the two duellers. Recognition was on her face.

"What? What is it?"

Scorpion frowned then shook her head.

"Do you know those guys?"

Again the frown and a slight tilt of her head to the side.

Then one of the fighters flashed his blade forwards and the other screamed as his sword hand parted company from its wrist.

"Enough of this! This ends now!" The wounded dueller shouted.

Dave strained to observe what was happening. There appeared to be a bright light emanating from the wounded dueller then the top of the mountain was consumed in the brightest light that the vampire had ever seen. He and Scorpion bent their heads down, instinctively covering their eyes from the ferocious glare.

Then…

…everything changed.

More constructs.

More angels.

Another battlefield.

This, however, was a different story. The angels seemed to be winning. They were driving the creatures of clay back. The winged warriors held up their hands and pulses of brilliant light flashed out, immobilising the constructs as if they were a Terracotta Army – glazed and polished, but ultimately useless.

Dave's brow creased as he watched the angels running in amidst their foes, smashing their solid forms apart and casting their desiccated remains to the wind. The sun shone high in the sky and baked the ground between the warring factions.

"Why did they not do this last time?"

Scorpion just shook her head. This was new to her. He saw no recognition on her face whatsoever.

And there, in the midst of the battle, one figure was claiming more construct kills than any other. Dave watched in fascination as a cowled figure danced and pirouetted between his foes, slashing left and right with a sword, cracking the air with a long whip which flashed silver at its tip in the bright sunshine. Not once could the vampire see the face of the animated fighter; some sort of cloth covered the warrior's face, preventing identification.

Yet, he knew him. He was sure of it. There was something familiar in this being's movements, the way he ran, the manner in which he leapt above his foe. It was as if the vampire had seen him before, in his dreams. As if he had run with him in the night.

Scorpion, too, was watching the battling stranger, her eyes locked on him in absolute wonder. Her mouth hung open at the grace and the ease with which he dispatched the constructs until, finally, not one remained.

"Claw!" Came a cry across the silent battlefield. "Claw!"

The being stood statuesque, his shoulders not moving the slightest from the heavy breathing that should have been necessary after such a feat, and raised his head.

"Claw…" The gnarled voice made Dave feel sick to his stomach.

He started as he realised that they no longer stood above the battlefield. Instead, they were in a place which he had visited once before.

A place he knew that he would visit again.

The place where he would die.

"That is the name that you go by now."

There it was again. That voice. A dead voice. An old voice.

A *familiar* voice.

It was the church. The decayed, ancient place of worship that had been transmuted into a realm of death. Dave looked up and caught sight of the eviscerated remains of some unfortunate pinned to the ceiling. He tore his eyes away before having to look at the dead unfortunate's tortured face, before being stung by the agony written in bold letters across his visage.

It had been a gothic church. There were pillars of stone lining the nave and the remains of wooden pews rotted where once a congregation of the faithful had sat. At the west end stood a font, a stone dish for baptism. Around its rim was an engraving: "Knaves are not our responsibility."

Dave frowned, both at the cryptic message and also at the noise that reached his ears. It was a soft singing, as if a shell was being held to his ear and the sea within was whispering a doleful lament. It called to him, wished for him to follow.

It was coming from the font.

It drew him towards it, held out its arms to embrace him.

Come to me, it soothed. *I am here. I will save you. Swim in my depths. I will make you whole again.*

He was oblivious to everything else: the hooded warrior who stood in the middle of the nave with his young companion behind him, the cloaked individual stooped over the dark altar at the east end of the church.

They meant nothing to him, whoever they were. He needed to approach the font. There was something there. Something which meant… What?

He did not know.

Come to me, the song repeated within his head. *I will make you what you are meant to be. I will tell you of such wondrous secrets. Listen to the marvels that I have seen.*

He found himself standing at the font as others discussed the fate of the universe. They were not his concern, not now, not yet.

He reached out, his fingers a hair's breadth from the stone of the bowl, and then there was a smaller set of digits in his other hand. His head turned and saw Scorpion holding his hand, her head shaking violently, but it was too late.

His fingers brushed the stone of the font.

And he was alive.

Not just a living, animated entity but truly, truly *alive*. His heart beat and his lungs flexed as he inhaled the dank stench of death from the crumbling church, but it was so much more than that. Everything was there, it all stood before him, ready to be taken and understood. It appeared as water, wet and translucent, but it burned like the fiercest of fires. It was a ball of intense light, like the sun in the sky that would fry him to a charred crisp. It pulsed and roared in front of his mental self. All he had to do was open his mouth, inhale and breathe it in.

Yes. Yes. Breathe me in. Let me empower your atrophied lungs. You will see such wonders. You will talk of many marvels. Things that have been yet are still to be shall dance upon your tongue.

Be my messenger.

Dave made to inhale…

Then there was a scream.

His mental head snapped to the left and saw Scorpion there, still clenching his hand, her skin scorched and burnt. Her long tresses were aflame like the cottage that they had previously visited. Her eyes were melting in their sockets.

No! No! He had done this. He could not let her die like this.

"Save her!" He screamed at the watery ball of burning knowledge. "I know you can! I know that I will lose you, but *save* her."

Are you sure? Would you spurn my knowledge, my gift, to spare this other?

"Yes! Please, now!"

You are truly remarkable. There was wonder in the entity's voice. *I am not sure that many others would do likewise.* Then it undulated away from him and encompassed the burning vampire. It spread out into a blanket of light, enveloping her screams of agony, her torched body, extinguishing the flames and renewing her charred flesh until it was, once more, a supple pink. Her eye sockets opened and it forced its way into the small orbs that solidified again from their glutinous mess until they were once more bright blue.

And *what* a blue!

Like the vast oceans, they were the azure of sky reflected in the deepest waters that held the greatest of knowledge.

Scorpion opened her mouth and, instead of agonised screams, there were words.

Then…

…everything changed.

"He who rose like a dragon of old shall be slain by the man of virtue."

Dave heard the soft words from the unfamiliar voice and opened his eyes. There was the smell of polish, beer and concerned onlookers.

There was also a quiet murmuring of confusion.

"Did… Did she just talk?"

"I don't know."

There was the noise of someone barging through the crowds. "Scorp! Cassie! Are you there?"

Dave felt a soft squeeze of his hand and looked over at the deep blue eyes that regarded him. "Thank you," they said without uttering a single syllable.

He squeezed the hand back and pulled himself to a sitting position.

"Are you okay?"

He smiled as he felt Nightingale's arm wrap around his shoulders. "Yes." He stretched his neck and felt his spine creak. "How long were we out?"

"Just seconds." Her eyes were pools of concern. "You just shook her hand, then you both collapsed."

"It felt like a lifetime. I have a lot to talk over with you."

Nightingale nodded.

"It'll have to wait," Marcus' deep baritone cut across the hubbub of the room. "Look."

All eyes in the bar shifted up to the widescreen plasma television on the wall where a number of faces, the likes of which you would not want to encounter in a dark alley, were being displayed. "In the following weeks," a precise female voice dictated, "more murders of known criminals have followed. Lancaster police…"

"Nightingale?"

The regent held a hand up for her son to be quiet.

"…have refused to comment on what local press are now calling the Vampire Vigilante."

The rest of the newscast was inaudible across the cries of disbelief in the bar.

"Nightingale. What is it? It can't be one of ours, can it? We don't do that."

Slumping down into a booth, Nightingale looked up at her child as she remembered words that had been spoken to her many, many years previous: *"When that day comes, I shall return."*

She looked up at her son, her companion, her subjects and words failed her.

Justice was back.

Scorpion
&
Tigress

Girls Just Wanna Have Fun

"Oh, this is just awesome!"

Derek Thompson let out a deep sigh as he realised that his uninterrupted run at filing Macintyre Papers' annual audits had just been terminally disturbed. He looked up from behind the mountain of buff coloured cardboard files and asked, with an air of resignation, "What is?"

His co-worker (Derek used the second part of that term quite loosely), Harry Dent, strode across the cramped office whilst slapping the back of his large hand against the pages of some trashy magazine. "This is, old boy! This splendid piece of stuff."

When it was thrust towards him, Derek took the glossy mag and gave it a cursory scan. It was the usual sort of drivel that so many of the younger office workers 'read'. Pages full of tits, cars and expensive watches. He had no time for that sort of thing. He was far too busy.

Thompson volunteered a non-committal shrug.

"That's it, old man?" boomed Dent. "A shrug?" He retrieved the magazine and flicked through it, looking for what Derek guessed Dent thought was a matter of importance. "You haven't even seen the little gem that I found." He paused and grinned. "Aha! Here we are!" and taking one of the large blue highlighters that he always seemed to have upon his bulky person, he scrolled a ring around something. "There you go, old man. Read it and weep."

Derek caught the magazine as it flew back across the desk towards him and scowled as he proceeded to read the highlighted section. The older man was rapidly losing patience with Dent's interruption. He ran his hand over his balding head which began to shake slowly when he saw that the text was the "Would like to meet" section. Once again, Dent was letting his favourite organ do his thinking for him.

"Two excitable young ladies looking for an experienced man who wants to try lots of new, fun things. We are both professional and intelligent so are looking for a man of similar social standing. Must be very open-minded and have great stamina. These girls just wanna have fun!" Good god. He could not be serious, surely? Even this was a step too far for the imbecile who got caught with his pants down in the reprographics room last month with that young typist from accounts. It was a miracle his fiancée had never found out.

Derek looked up from the magazine into the beaming, ruddy face of his co-worker.

"Well, old man?"

"What about Margaret?"

Dent waved a dismissive paw as if the subject was irrelevant. "Oh, don't be such a fuddy-duddy. You know we have an," his tongue slithered across his lips, "open relationship."

By that, Derek knew that Dent meant he got to play away as often as he liked, but if some chap so much as looked at his woman he would let all his rugby-playing weight pound that man into the ground.

Derek tried another tack. "It's a set up."

Dent looked bemused, "Don't get you, old fella."

"You have no idea who these girls are or what they're after."

Dent bellowed a raucous guffaw. "Hah! They're hot and they're after the time of their lives!"

"How can you be sure, Harry? What if they lure you to some seedy joint and then an accomplice nips out and mugs you? Hmmm? Have you thought about that?"

Dent raised his ginger eyebrows. "Mug me? Me? The biggest hunk of muscle that ever stacked files in the archives? I think not, old man. I'd grab these totties by the neck, pin them to the floor, then, when they could smell my rampant testosterone filling their noses, I'd give their longing mouths exactly what they wanted."

Derek sighed for what seemed to be the hundredth time in the last five minutes. "Okay," he said, handing the magazine back; "if you say so, Harry."

"I do indeed, old man. Now if you'll excuse me I have a phone-call to make."

Okay. Okay.

Calm down. It's cool. *You're* cool. You know that.

What's the time? Eight fifty-five. Okay. We said nine, so that's cool. Five minutes early. Nice cold beer. Ice cold beer. Have a sip. Have a sip.

There that's better. Damn, tastes good.

Shit shit shit. Why am I so damn nervous?

Still eight fifty-five. Stop looking at your bloody watch. It'll make it go quicker.

More beer. Yes, beer. Good old beer.

Okay. Okay.

Five minutes.

Then show-time!

Ha!

Can't believe it. Can't bloody believe it, man. She sounded so hot, didn't she? Sexy voice. So sexy.

Hope she has a nice arse. Hope they both do. Like a nice arse, don't we? Oh, yes we do.

It's hot in here. Yes, so hot.

That's better. Open collar now. Yeah, bit cooler.

More beer.

Am I sweating? Am I? No. Don't think so. My pits are dry.

Nice bar. Not been here before. No United supporters. Wankers. So up themselves. City rock!

More beer.

Where are they?

Eight fifty-eight.

Okay. Still a bit early, I guess.

Are they coming, though? Second thoughts?

Nah. Course not. She didn't sound like the sort to have second thoughts.

I have got the right bar, haven't I?

Course I have. See, there it is. Yeah. That's where I am. Yeah. Right bar.

Nine pm. Stop looking at your watch! They'll be here.

What did she say they looked like again? Red and blonde? Yeah, red and blonde. Sure she said blonde? Not brunette? Yeah, blonde. Blonde. She said blonde.

Red and blonde.

Nice.

I'm sat in the right place.

Yeah, right place. At the back of the bar. Discreet.

One past nine. Shit shit shit. They're late. They're late. They're not coming.

Course they are, you dumb fuck. Course they are.

Two of 'em. Shit. Two of 'em. Hah! Wasn't the old man jealous? Baldy couldn't pull two hotties.

Uh uh. No way.

I could though.

And I have.

Oh yeah.

Oh yeah.

Oh... shit!

That's them isn't it? At the bar. How'd I miss them? Blonde and Red. Getting drinks.

Fuck! What do I do? Do I go up to 'em? No. No. What if it's not them? God, I'd get slapped! Ha! Perv alert. No. No. Wait a minute. They said here. If it's them, they'll come here. Yeah. They'll come here.

Just wait.

Chill.

Be cool.

More beer.

Yes! It's them. Red's seen me. Talking to Blonde. Nodding.

Here they come.

Oh, you jammy bastard!

"Hey there," it was Red who was speaking. Blonde was stood just behind her companion, peering curiously over the redhead's shoulder. "You Harry?"

Dent was momentarily paralysed as his brain tried to assimilate what his unbelieving eyes were seeing. Both girls were about five-foot-six-ish. Red had the most vividly coloured hair he had ever come across, cut quite short and spiky, letting him fully take in her emerald eyes and pixie-shaped nose. Blonde's hair cascaded down her back and Dent could see it flowing round behind her arse. She had deep, sapphire blue eyes and a very slim mouth. Both wore short, short skirts revealing an incredible amount of slender leg, and both had very tight fitting vest tops, showing off tattoos on their left shoulders: Red a tiger, Blonde a scorpion.

All Dent could do was sit and gawp. Christmas had come early this year.

Red raised a slim, sculpted eye-brow. "Cat got your tongue or we got the wrong guy?"

"What?" Dent snapped out of his reverie, "No! No! Shit no. I'm Harry." He shot up, almost sending his beer flying. He thrust a warm hand out to them. "Pleased to meet you. Very pleased."

Red took his hand. Harry thought he would either cum or faint right there. Her touch was so light and sensuous. "Pleased to meet you too, Harry." Her friend just smiled from behind a veil of blonde hair. "Scorpion's pleased to meet you too."

"Scorpion?"

Red pointed to Blonde's tattoo, "She's Scorpion," then her own, "and I'm Tigress. May we sit down?"

"Of course. Of course. Please, take a seat."

Tigress lowered herself down onto the sofa and lifted her feet up onto the low table. Harry couldn't help but stare at the soft, white skin that belonged to her legs. Keeping her cocktail in her left hand, she patted the seat next to her with her right and smiled up at Dent. He dutifully sat down. "Good boy, Harry," she purred and ran a finger down the side of his cheek. He felt the firm caress of the finger-tip followed by the quick scrape of the long, painted nail. He stopped himself from gasping.

Scorpion silently folded herself into the seat on his right side, tucking her legs underneath her and pushing up close to him. Harry turned to watch her. "Hi," he squeaked.

The blonde just pulled her Rapunzel-like locks around over her shoulder and continued to smile at him.

"Don't mind her," Tigress whispered conspiratorially, "she don't say much."

Harry could feel the warmth of her breath caressing his ear and the scent of their combined perfumes were dancing in his nostrils. More beer. Quickly.

As the cold liquid trickled down his gullet towards his stomach, he felt himself start to relax. Yeah. He was cool. He was good at this. He was the Dentster. "So, what is it you ladies do then?"

Scorpion giggled coquettishly. "Oh we do lots of things Harry," Tigress breathed. "Lots of *nice* things."

More beer.

"I, er... meant, what do you do for... a ... living?"

Tigress was eyeing him appreciatively over the rim of her cocktail. "We're *researchers*, Harry."

"Researchers? What in?"

"Whatever we get told to do by our boss. He commands it and it is done. What do you do, Harry?"

Dent held her gaze, his confidence building. "I'm in accounts. At Macintyre Papers."

"Wow," Tigress sipped her drink and showed real admiration. "Paper, hey? Where would we be without it? Such an important job, Harry."

"Damn right," Harry could feel his courage really starting to mount now. "People don't realise just how important paper is. Paper-less society my arse! We'd be screwed without the stuff."

"Oh, that is *sooo* true, Harry."

Harry couldn't help but notice that the long legs had left the table and were now crossed over and rubbing slowly against his. Divine.

"I do admire men who undertake such *important* work. And an *accountant* too? You must be good with figures."

"I sure am. Best in the office."

"And how about *your* figure, Harry?" Tigress continued to purr, her soft leg now slipping half over his, and her nose nuzzling at his ear, "Is your figure nice, my love?"

This was incredible! Dent could feel his cock starting to rise so fast that he was sure the girls must be able to see the bulge in his trousers. "Yeah. Yeah. I work out at the weekends. Play rugby too. Gotta keep trim," he chuckled.

"Mmmm. Mmmm... Nice... Scorpion likes nice toned abs, don't you, Scorp?"

Harry turned to the blonde and Scorpion nodded as she slipped her hand over his stomach, starting to unfasten a couple of shirt buttons. He let out a short gasp as she slipped her delicate fingers inside the crisp cotton fabric. God it felt so good!

Slowly, she worked her hand round and round over the smooth skin of his tense stomach, searching and probing as she drew nearer. Then she took his ear-lobe in her mouth. Dent sighed as she tugged at it whilst emitting out a soft, throaty growl.

Tigress' knees rose higher up the inside of Dent's leg as she gently scolded her blonde companion, "Now, now girlfriend. Behave yourself. There'll be plenty of time for that later." She purposefully placed her drink down on the table then ran her hand over Dent's thigh and up between his legs, gently letting one finger trace his excited bulge, before grasping round Scorpion's wrist and drawing her hand away. "We mustn't be too forward, must we? Don't want to scare the kind Mister Dent." Then, taking the blonde by her hand, she stood up, "Please excuse us Harry, but we need to go powder each other's noses." Blowing him a kiss, they turned and left Dent gawping at the perfectly shaped arses that sauntered through the bar to the ladies' toilets.

Tigress meticulously scrubbed her hands in the basin and looked over at Scorpion, "Well?"

Scorpion nodded.

"You're sure?"

Scorpion nodded again, her long hair cascading over her shoulders.

After drying her hands, Tigress touched up her lipstick without once looking in the mirror, then turned back to her old friend. "Okay. Let's do it."

The three of them went back to his place. Harry Dent was rather proud of his bachelor pad. He worked damn hard, so he spent his wages well. On the wall in the living room was a huge LED TV. He had all the decent channels of course. Next to it was a multimedia centre that had set him back well over two grand. He flicked it on with the remote and soft music drifted through the apartment. It was something from the early nineties. Warm. Erotic. Oh yeah, baby, get it on. He suffered a mild moment of annoyance when he saw the answer-phone flashing at him accusatively. He huffed as he flicked it on whilst dimming the lights.

It was Margaret.

"Hi Sweetie! Only me."

So I can hear, he thought.

"Tried your mobile, but I think you've turned it off."

No shit?

"Anyways, I know you're *sooo* busy with work tonight. Just wanted to say I wuv woo." There was the sound of a huge, wet kiss and the phone clicked off.

If her old man wasn't so loaded...

Dent's thoughts were interrupted by the sound of soft movement from behind him. He turned and saw the blonde beauty regarding him with a faint, knowing smile and twinkling azure eyes before she wandered off to join her girlfriend in the kitchen.

"*Excellent!*" came the happy voice of Tigress, "You don't mind me opening this champers do you Harry, sweetie?"

He heard the cork pop open on a five-hundred pound bottle of vintage champagne. He should have protested, but he wouldn't. No. Not tonight. Not at all.

Some glasses of Bollinger and a large whiskey later, the three of them were in Harry's bedroom. Dent stood and looked at the two beauties in front of him, curled up on his bed, slowly stroking each other whilst sipping more champagne. They had removed their shoes and skirts and were now just wearing their knickers and vests. Harry had a very good idea that there was nothing on underneath those vests. He finished his whiskey and began to undo his shirt.

Scorpion giggled and whispered something in Tigress' ear. Red smiled as she sipped some more champagne.

"What'd she say?"

"Oh, she just commented that I'll love your nice smooth tummy," Tigress purred, eyeing Harry up and down hungrily — every bit her namesake. She beckoned with a long finger. "Come here. Let us help you."

Dent stumbled towards the bed on leaden legs. He felt rather flushed from the booze. The girls guided him down onto his back and began to strip his shirt off. He closed his eyes as he felt one of them (he couldn't tell which) begin to kiss down his chest and over his belly as his arms were pulled from the shirt.

"Mmmm..." came the voice (so it was Tigress doing the kissing then); "Yes, she's so right. What a tasty one you are. And such a smooth, flat tummy too." Harry groaned as her tongue roamed around his waistline. "Don't see many folks with no belly-button do you? You lose it, Harry?"

"C...can't remember, oh god, ever having one," he stammered as Scorpion joined in the kissing. "Didn't know my parents, *jesusjesusjesus*. Must have been a test-tube baby or summat."

He felt the kissing stop. Dent opened his eyes and saw them looking at each other over the top of him. "What's the matter?"

Tigress turned to him and smiled. "Oh, we were just wondering if you'd like some *special treatment* Harry? What do you think?"

Dent's head bounced up and down against the pillow as he nodded rapidly, "Oh yes! Please, yes!" he shouted.

Blondie slipped off the bed and sidled over to where her purse had been thrown along with her skirt. There was a muffled jangling noise, then she came back dangling two pairs of handcuffs on an index finger.

Dent's mouth hung open wide enough to fit a train inside. "For... for you?" he asked.

Scorpion and Tigress beamed widely as they shook their heads. Scorpion passed one pair to her friend and the two of them ran the cold metal shackles up over Harry's chest to his arms. Then, grabbing one wrist each in unison, they snapped the cuffs shut, first to him, then to the bedstead.

"So... you girls do this a lot then?" he asked as he tugged his arms against the cuffs. No give. None whatsoever.

"Oh, all the time Harry," Tigress replied as she went back to kissing his chest momentarily before sipping some more wine. "Mmmm... This is a good vintage. What year was it again?"

Harry had his eyes blissfully shut and barely whispered, "1900."

"Ah. I loved 1900. Year of the Boxer Rebellion. That was a good year."

133

Harry felt the sensual sliding of material and skin over his belly as Scorpion whispered something to Tigress.

Tigress laughed, "No honey, they didn't have champagne back in 60." More whispering. "Oh, sorry. You meant you liked the *year*. Yes, Boudicca was fun, wasn't she?"

Boudicca.

Alarm bells started to ring in Harry's head. Boudicca? 60? 1900? His eyes flashed open. What greeted him immediately parched his throat.

Teeth. Two sets of very sharp teeth.

Seeing the look on his face, Tigress placed her empty glass on the bed-stand and ran her finger slowly down one of her fangs. "Oh, Harry. I'd say we were sorry and that we don't like doing this to you," she shrugged nonchalantly, "but then I'd be a liar, wouldn't I?" Turning to the other vampire, "You wanna go first this time, Scorp? I know wine always gives you an appetite."

A little while later, Tigress was simultaneously dabbing her lover's cheek with a piece of tissue whilst talking on her mobile.

"Yeah, we're done here.

"Nope, no problems. Hold still, sweetie.

"Not you! Scorp got a bit messy."

She stuck her tongue out at her partner.

"Uh huh. Yeah. Right. Okay."

She stopped cleaning the other vampire up and mimed nagging movements with her hand.

Scorpion placed her delicate hands over her mouth and stifled a giggle.

"Look, honey. We've been doing this long before your ancestors ever made it to Britain, okay?

"I know. I know. You just want to make sure we get the right ones. Well, needless to say, Harry-boy was navel free. No sign of a natural birth.

"Yes. That too. He tasted of clay. Definitely a construct.

"Okay, that's fine. Catch you later."

Scorpion mimed a little wave.

"Oh, Scorp says 'Bye'. He says 'Bye' back atcha."

She hung up and snapped the little phone shut. "Okay babe, let's get dressed and hit the town. The night's still young."

Scorpion smiled and linked her arm through Tigress' as they exited the flat and left discarded on the bed the desiccated remains of the late Harry "biggest hunk of muscle that ever stacked files in the archives" Dent.

They were off for some more fun.

Memento

Darting rain stung the apparently young woman's chilled flesh as she hurtled through the dark woods at a speed unimaginable by those who pursued her. Dishevelled long blonde hair clung to her scalp and her neck as she paused briefly to listen to the night. Her hyper-acute senses detected no more than woodland creatures scurrying down into the protective earth to escape the accursed precipitation.

The woman scowled. She hated rain almost as much as she despised those who she had lost by weaving in and out of the trees and shadows of the dense forest. The land where she had spent her formative youth had been far warmer. Hot sun had baked fine sand and the water she had known had been the warm lapping of the Mediterranean at her toes as she had paddled as a child, hunting for shells.

This country, however, was the epitome of wet. It rained almost all the time, and when there was no rain there was the continual reek of mould and effluent.

Did its inhabitants not know how to bathe?

She really had no idea how her partner could have endured it for so many centuries.

The woman shifted the dead weight on her shoulder as she let her senses roam her surroundings. No, the noises of her pursuers had faded away into the far distance. However, there was something else.

Smoke.

The fragrant aroma of a hearth.

Even with her unusual strength, the woman was tired from carrying her burden, a burden that needed rest and recuperation. What to do? Should she try and find somewhere dry in what appeared to be the wettest place on the gods' earth or should she risk the charity of strangers?

She shifted her load one more time and frowned as her hand came away soaked in blood.

Strangers it would have to be.

If they protested, she could always kill them.

Nathan was a man of simple means. His modest hut in the middle of the woods provided him with the privacy that he required for his art. No one ever visited him because, apart from those who collected his heavier wares, no one could ever find him. If he needed the contact of others for food or for trade, he would climb into his rickety old cart and ride the winding distance to the nearest village. Quietly and conscientiously he tapped at his chisel that was carving out the final touches to his latest work: a misericord for a church somewhere far away. He had no idea where, nor did he care. Men with money paid him well to create things of beauty. His life, he felt was idyllic.

Except for one thing.

Laying his tools down on his bench he peered over at another misericord which he had yet to start and tugged pensively at his chin. So far, he had completed four and was almost finished on the fifth. The sixth pew seat, however, sat there blankly regarding him in the exact same manner as a sullen hound awaiting some tasty scraps from the table.

He had no idea what to carve upon its wood.

Normally, the designs just presented themselves. He would wake in the morning and there they would be ready in his head as if they had been fermenting like a good ale overnight. He would pick up his tools, go to work and produce an object of serene beauty. This seat, however, was being stubborn. Nothing was coming to mind.

"What am I to do, my friend?" he sighed, turning around to regard his silent companion. The carver eased himself up from his table and approached the huge stone statue that dominated the far end of his workshop. Its empty stone orbs gazed vacantly into the room as Nathan ran an affectionate hand over one of its curled wings. "I don't know," he smiled, "never any advice." Then he chuckled and poured himself a draught of ale from the barrel that rested next to the grotesque. "None of this for you, then." He winked mischievously and was about to taste the drink when there was a hurried knocking at the door. The mason frowned. "Expecting anyone?" he asked his creation.

The statue remained resolutely silent.

"Must be for me then," he muttered as he walked over to the entrance to his cottage.

On opening the door there was an explosion of rain, blonde hair and dishevelled clothing as a young woman fell through the doorway with a companion slung over her shoulder. The stranger turned, glanced at Nathan, looked as if she were about to say something then promptly passed out on the floor.

The solitary workman looked at the two beautiful women unconscious at his feet and said to his silent companion, "Well that's not something I see every day."

They were coming for her. She could hear their relentless feet crashing through the night.

"Scorpion! Quick, this way!"

She turned and saw her friend, her companion, her creator, her lover, Tigress, beckoning for her to follow, gesturing with an outstretched hand.

Scorpion picked her feet up to follow but it was as if they were mired in mud.

In clay.

She looked down and saw wet viscous hands oozing up out of the ground, slithering up her legs and pulling her down. Desperately, she reached out to her lover but her hands dropped as she saw the redhead slumped down on the floor, blood gushing from her middle.

There was nothing she could do. They had her and they were dragging her down.

The hands methodically inched their way up her back, their clammy fingers prodding and probing as they encompassed her body.

She felt a hand touch her shoulder and gently shake her.

Her blue eyes snapped open and she grabbed the hand in a vice.

There was cursing from its owner.

Scorpion ignored the expletives and quickly scanned her immediate surroundings. It was the cottage that she had seen in the forest. She had carried Tigress here and entered before there had been the dream.

Tigress had been hurt.

Tigress!

She thrust the hand away and its owner clattered to the floor. Scorpion turned to see her lover lying aside her in bed. She appeared peaceful, asleep, but exceptionally pale.

The blonde woman grabbed her friend's shoulders and started to vigorously shake her back and forth. Tigress' head bounced rhythmically up and down on the bedlinen but the redhead did not respond.

"Your friend is gravely hurt," came a voice.

Scorpion spun around and glared at its source.

"Careful, careful. She was like that when you arrived two nights ago."

It was a man, about forty by the looks of him. Light brown hair, a stubbled chin and dark brown eyes that watched her carefully from behind outstretched protective hands that bore workman's callouses on the fingers.

Scorpion inhaled deeply. Aside from smells of woodsmoke, dust, freshly carved timber and stone, there was just flesh and blood. He was human.

Harmless.

For now.

She ignored him and returned her attention to her companion. Softly, the blonde woman ran her fingers down an ice cold cheek. Shaking her head, she lifted the bedding to check on Tigress' wound. What she saw made her gasp. It was not just the ferocity of the deep gash that stretched across her lover's mid-rift but the fact that she was completely naked.

It was then that Scorpion realised that she too was not wearing a single stitch of clothing.

Nathan watched carefully as the woman realised that someone had removed her clothes. This was not good.

"So, let's not lose our temper now. Your garments were damaged and covered in blood." He spoke quickly as she paced towards him. "I took them off to clean them. Look, they are over there, repaired." He pointed frantically at the pile of clothing on the stool in the corner of the room, causing the woman to halt her murderous advance. She shot the clothes a quick look and stared back at him again before marching over and grabbing her tunic. Nathan felt himself flush as it dropped over her lithe body.

Once dressed, the blonde gave him an awkward little nod before returning to her companion.

"Don't mention it," Nathan managed as his heart rate started to calm back down. He maintained a cautious distance as the woman knelt quietly on the bed and went back to stroking her companion. "She looks very ill. I'm not sure that I can help her any more. I stitched the wound together as best as I could." Slowly, like a man approaching a wild beast that had wandered in to warm itself by his fire, he walked around the bed. Carefully, in order to protect the redhead's modesty, the mason pulled back the bedclothes to reveal his unconventional handiwork. "See, nice and neat, but I think she needs help from the village."

The blonde ran a slender finger over the puckered wound and shook her head, then looked up at Nathan and repeated the gesture once again, this time more assertively.

"But she could die!" he protested.

The corner of the blonde's mouth curled up into a curious little smile as, once more, her head slowly moved from side to side.

The man was no threat, of that Scorpion was sure. He had taken them both in with no question, cleaned and mended their garments and, bless him, had tried to save Tigress' life.

If only he knew. She could not help but smile.

The wound was savage and definitely needed treating, but not by a mortal quack nor a physician. She looked up at the man again and considered what needed doing. She did not think he would panic, nevertheless she reached out and gently gave his warm hand a quick squeeze before placing a single finger to her lips.

He understood and nodded.

Scorpion nodded back then took her wrist to her mouth and bit down hard. There was a small gasp from the man and she raised her blonde eyebrows at him.

"Sorry," he apologised.

She turned back to Tigress and let the blood from her wrist trickle across her lover's wound. As it did so, she rubbed it into the gash with a finger. Gently, she worked the life-giving liquid back and forth until her own flesh-wound began to heal. Absentmindedly, she licked at her wrist with her tongue, not wasting a drop and, as she did so, Tigress' wound began to writhe under the blood. Scorpion was aware of the man drawing closer and watching open-mouthed as she continued to massage the fluid into Tigress' flesh. Then, when it had all been absorbed, she tugged gently at the crude thread that their saviour had used two nights previous and slowly prised it out, leaving behind fresh, smooth skin.

She looked up at the man and her blue eyes twinkled in the firelight.

"Marvellous," he gasped from behind a wide smile.

Scorpion grinned back at him.

He leaned in closer and his hand warily approached the smooth, healed skin. "May I?" he asked.

Scorpion nodded as she absentmindedly ran her fingers through the unconscious woman's hair.

The man's hand gently traced a line where only a moment ago a vicious life-threatening wound had cut a deep groove. "Truly amazing. A wondrous thing." His voice was no more than a whisper. "She is so cold." Scorpion smiled to herself as he drew the bedclothes up around her partner. It was not necessary, but again it illustrated his kindness.

There was a loud growling from the man's stomach. "Oh!" he exclaimed. "It appears that I am hungry. Would you like to eat?"

Scorpion gave him another quiet smile.

"Or should that be, *do* you eat?"

The woman's smile widened as she gave him an affirmative nod. True, she did not *need* to eat, but to refuse the kindness of this nice man would be rude. Quietly, she followed him over to a small wooden table. There was just one chair. "I'm not used to entertaining," he explained, offering the battered seat to his unusual guest. "I shall fetch myself a stool."

Scorpion let her eyes gaze around the room. The best word to describe it was *functional.* On one side was the bed, a simple wooden affair with plain linen. Then there was the small table for dining, although, judging by the tools dotted about it, it served as a type of workbench too. Then, past the fire, was the workshop proper. Her keen eyesight flitted from various woodcarvings up to a huge winged beast that resided by the far wall.

The man came back to the table juggling two bowls of something that he had spooned out from a pot on the fire. "You like him?"

Scorpion nodded quickly before tasting the concoction in the bowl. Gods it was vile, but she pretended it was the most delicious thing she had ever tasted so as not to offend her attentive host.

"I was commissioned to carve about a dozen of them for a church somewhere up north," the man explained. "The others have already gone but there wasn't enough room for him on the carts, so they are collecting him next month. It's funny, but I feel that he watches me all the time. Not in a sinister manner but in some sort of curious fashion. I feel that he needs a name, you know? He has a personality. But I just cannot think of what to call him.

"Oh!" he slapped his hand to his forehead. "Where are my manners? I haven't properly introduced myself." He hastily wiped his right hand on his smock before thrusting it out. "I am Nathan. Very pleased to meet you."

Scorpion took his hand and gave it a quick shake, watching his eyes as they felt her skin.

"Your friend is not the only one who is chilled to the bone."

Scorpion shrugged.

"May I enquire as to what *your* name is?"

She placed the bowl of noxious gloop down on the table and rolled up her sleeve to show the tattoo that adorned her shoulder.

Nathan frowned. "What manner of beast is that? It looks like a spider, but it has a tail like a lance."

Scorpion frowned. This was somewhat frustrating. She mimed for writing implements and Nathan fetched a piece of charcoal and a thin slip of wood. She wrote her name down for him to see and he looked at it as if he was a monkey examining the intricacies of a plough.

"I'm sorry," the carver apologised, "reading is not my strong point. I just carve."

Scorpion let out a long puff of exasperation and looked over her shoulder to her sleeping companion. What she would give for her mouthpiece to be up and about right now!

Three days passed and, as they did, Scorpion started to relax into her new found domestic situation. Nathan was an impeccable host, providing her with a warm bed (which she shared with the still unconscious Tigress), stimulating conversation and less than edible food. Unable to be parted from her lover, she never left the hut but busied herself by studying the skills that the craftsman utilised in his work.

"It's like this," he explained one morning as he whittled away on a small piece of timber, "I feel that I have to create life, you know? I take this inanimate object and, with my hands and tools, I breathe vitality into it. It may not walk or talk, but when people look at it, they can feel it breathe. The hairs stand up on the nape of their neck and they truly believe that my work has a soul. Like that fellow over there," he motioned to the grotesque. "One day, he will stand with his companions above a thriving city and people shall look up, knowing that he watches over them. They will see the stone statue, but they will feel the living, thinking creature."

Scorpion looked over at the statue and she knew exactly what Nathan meant. It really was as if those blank eyes were watching her and taking in every detail.

So it continued until on the fourth morning, shortly after daybreak, an unfamiliar noise crept into the room.

"*Cassie...*"

There was a blonde blur as one moment Scorpion was stood hovering over Nathan's shoulder, then the next she was knelt on the bed holding her lover's cold hand.

"*There you are...*" came the frail voice, "*my beautiful Trojan.*"

The blonde woman pressed the redhead's hand to her mouth and covered it in kisses.

"Missed me?" Tigress' voice gained strength as her green eyes twinkled and she pulled herself up to a sitting position. "Where are..?" Her voice trailed off as she spied Nathan hovering in the background.

Scorpion felt her lover's body tense into flight or fight. She cupped a hand around the seated woman's cheek and turned her head upwards. Smiling, she shook her head.

Tigress studied her partner's eyes and began to relax. "He's good?"

Scorpion nodded, her blonde hair falling around her face.

The redhead reached up and tucked a stray hair behind the blonde's ear. "If you say so." Then she turned to their host. "Greetings! I'm Tigress.

You got any ale? I feel like a hog has been using my throat for a latrine."

Nathan's paralysis broke as he hurried over with a wooden cup of liquid. "Pleased to meet you. I am Nathan. Your companion brought you here a few days ago. You were gravely ill. She nursed you back to health."

Tigress glugged down the contents of the cup. "Gods, that's good! That's my Scorpion, always dragging me out of danger."

"Scorpion." Nathan felt the texture of the new name roll around his mouth. "That is the creature you have on your arm?" he asked the blonde.

"Sure is," the redhead answered. "And this is me," she pointed to the fierce-looking tattoo on her respective shoulder. "We got two for the price of one some years ago." She chuckled at the perplexed look on the carver's face. "You don't get out much, do you?"

Nathan shrugged. "Nor do I entertain much. Oh! You must be starving. Would you like something to eat?"

Tigress gave Scorpion a curious frown as the blonde chuckled quietly to herself.

It had been so quiet: Nathan thought to himself as he carefully engraved a rose onto the rim of a wooden plate that he had been toying with. When it had been just him and Scorpion, it had felt like not much had changed. Life had more or less carried on as normal. There had been no incessant chatter, no raucous laughter and no random assortment of clothing distributed around his small home. When the two women had arrived, the only clothes they had possessed were the ones in which they had been dressed. However, since Tigress had awoken, there seemed to be random heaps of female clothes appearing around the place. It was as if she mysteriously magicked them out of thin air.

When he asked them what certain articles were, Nathan just nodded politely in complete befuddlement as the excitable redhead listed off long exotic names for items the purpose of which he could not even begin to imagine.

This was not to say that he did not like her. Far from it. She was more intoxicating than the strongest ale he had ever quaffed. Late into the night, she would tell tales of far off lands where she and Scorpion had stood back to back, battling foes of overwhelming numbers, always to emerge victorious and dripping in the spoils of war.

"I guess we just got over-confident," she admitted one night, idly spinning her wooden cup between her hands. "We thought we were invincible. It almost got us killed."

Nathan watched as Scorpion placed a hand on her partner's wrist and emphatically shook her head.

"I know. I know that's not possible. Not here, not now. We both know how it ends for us," Tigress mused, the weight of the world in her voice. "It's just, it felt so close. Death was snapping at our heels and, as I felt darkness grab me, I began to wonder if what I saw when I was created was wrong. Silly, I know."

"When you were *created*?"

For the first time since she had awoken from her wound, Tigress was still, silent.

"It's okay," Nathan reassured her. "I know that you are not like me, like other people. I have seen you healed from a wound that should have claimed your life. I have seen that you do not leave this hut during the daytime." He smiled, "I have seen you surreptitiously discard your food into the fire. You are not human, are you?"

"No, we're not," Tigress said, the flickering of the fire making her eyes gleam like the finest emeralds. "We were once, just like you. But that was many, many years ago. We have watched empires rise and fall yet we still carry on doing what we do."

"And what would that be?"

The woman's hand subconsciously stroked where she had been wounded. "Kill those who would see us slaughtered." She looked over at the blonde and unspoken words flew between them before she continued, "There is a war, Nathan, the likes of which you would never imagine. It has been simmering away in the cooking pot of history since certain ingredients were added at the dawn of time and we are just foot soldiers doing our duty. There are creatures out there that look like you and talk like you. They wear your clothes and eat your food, yet they have no soul. They are monstrosities created by some malign force to infiltrate your world and hunt down those which stand against that belief which these monsters hold firm to in their inhuman hearts."

"And what, may I ask, *is* that belief?" the carver inquired.

Tigress looked him squarely in the eyes. "That the human race is an abhorrence and needs to be eradicated and that those which would be its saviours must be located and destroyed."

Nathan sat back on his stool and frowned. "By saviours, do you mean those like you?"

Both of the women slowly shook their heads.

"No," Tigress said, a distant look in her eyes. "Not us. But it is our job to find them." There was a pause and then she said, "But in the meantime, do you have any more of that ale?"

A few days later, a cart rattled down the overgrown path to Nathan's cottage. The carver was busying himself by the fire with a pot of vile-smelling liquid which he explained to his guests was a preservative to be applied to his wooden creations to stop them from rotting.

Tigress peered into the noxious gloop and feigned vomiting. "You mean that men of the cloth will be perching their pious posteriors on this rancid brew?"

Nathan chuckled. "By the time it dries, it will not smell as bad. By the time they have been installed, there will be no trace of it remaining."

"Shame," Tigress grinned, "it would cover their pompous flatulence."

The two of them were laughing and Scorpion was smiling when there was a hammering at the door.

"Ah!" cried out the craftsman, "Time for our friend to depart." He crossed the room and opened the door. There on the threshold was a rough-looking man of average height.

"Are you the mason?"

"Yes, yes. Come in. Come in."

As the newcomer entered the building, his nose wrinkled. "What is that awful stench?"

"Apparently it's to protect some seats from pious posteriors," Tigress called out.

The man's eyes flicked across the room to the bubbling pot then to the two women stood next to it. He frowned and grunted. "It burns my nose. Where's the statue?" He enquired.

Nathan led him to the grotesque, which had been bound onto a trolley ready to be moved.

"Ugly brute, isn't he?"

Scorpion cast her partner a frown.

Tigress just raised an eyebrow.

"Beauty is what's within us," Nathan said as he helped the rude man wheel the statue out of the room. "It can be found in the smallest and the largest thing."

They grunted and strained as they heaved the dead weight up onto the cart before lashing it down tight. The carter tossed the mason his payment before peering back into the cottage. "In my opinion, some things are just vile to the core." He climbed up onto his seat, cracked his reins and the cart trundled off into the forest.

Sweat covered Nathan's body and his throat felt infernally tight. He gasped frantically as he woke with a start.

"Careful, careful. Calm down."

His head darted left and right as a cool pair of hands held him and soft words soothed him.

"Calm. Calm. It was a nightmare."

"The beasts!" he wailed when his throat finally loosened. "They burnt the ground! Everywhere. Fire!" Then he felt himself drawn close to a chest and inhaled a sweet female scent as Tigress held him tight.

"It's over. It's over," she soothed. "Just a dream."

He wrapped his arms around her and sobbed into her shoulder like a child that had seen its pet hound killed by a boar. "It was so real. So real." When the man had calmed down, he pulled away and rubbed the back of his hand across his wet eyes. "I am so sorry. What must you think of me?"

"That's okay." The redhead kept a comforting hand on his knee. "Scorp has dreams too, you know? Some of them are, well, quite useful."

Scorpion nodded as she too placed a reassuring hand on the distraught man.

"Useful?"

The women nodded as Tigress explained. "Sometimes she sees the future. When she was younger no one ever believed her — some sort of curse — but now... Well it's gotten us out of quite a few situations."

The carver looked from one of the women to the other, then back again. "I sincerely hope that dream never comes true."

"Want to tell us what it was?"

He screwed up his face trying to recall the nightmare. "I can't remember all of it, but I will never forget the heat. Everywhere was burning! The trees were aflame and the ground was scorched. And there was the most monstrous noise, like denizens of hell calling the damned to their wretched fate. I tried to block my ears but could not protect myself from the horrible sound.

"Then I saw its source. There were two dragons, one red and one black. I think the red one had many heads. They were fighting and, as they did, the ground shook and creatures rose from its depths. They were abhorrent! Their skin was brown like dirt and they had no faces that I could distinguish, just mouths that stretched from one side of their head to the other. As the dragons fought, these creatures turned and advanced on me. I knew they wanted to feast on me..."

He trailed off, the looks of concern on the women's faces drawing him to a halt.

"These are the creatures that you fight, aren't they?"

The silence confirmed that they were.

"Why did I dream that? Why did I see such things? Normally, I dream of things of beauty. When I awake, I carve them into wood or stone. I cannot bring these monstrosities to life!"

"We are so sorry, Nathan." Tigress' voice was very quiet. "We have brought our world into yours." She slipped an arm around her partner and their heads touched sorrowfully. "We will pack our things and leave."

Nathan stared at the two curious women in their loving embrace and gasped in realisation. "No! No! You mustn't leave." He scrambled from where he had been sleeping and scurried across to his work tools. "No, not yet, anyways." He grabbed the blank misericord and hefted it up onto his work table before scratching rapidly at its bare surface with a sharp implement.

Tigress gave Scorpion a bemused frown.

Scorpion returned her lover's confusion with a shrug.

For the next few hours, the craftsman was in his own little world and heaven help anyone who interrupted him. He had positioned the misericord in such a manner that neither of his houseguests could see what he was creating. All they observed was the master at work, chiselling, scribing, sanding, occasionally standing back to view his work in progress and muttering to himself. Once, Scorpion took him a cup of ale for refreshment. He impolitely snatched it out of her hand and shooed her away much to the amusement of Tigress, who was reclining on the bed, propped up on her elbow.

Eventually, it was apparent that Nathan had finished. He was lovingly applying some of the vile-smelling preservative to the wood and whistling tunelessly to himself. Then, he stood back, smiled and beckoned for the women to come and view his handiwork. When they did, Scorpion was not the only one who was speechless.

"Well?" he asked with the anxiety of all artists. "What do you think?"

Both of the women flung their arms around him, hugged him and covered his head in kisses.

"My, my," the maestro stammered, "I am guessing that you like it."

"Nathan, it's so beautiful!" Tigress lavished praise on the seat as she let her fingers hover over the intricate carvings, first of Scorpion's face, then her own. "It's so real, so lifelike." There in front of her was an exact reproduction of the two of them embracing. Also, under the respective lovers, were carved delicate representations of a scorpion and a tiger. It was impossible not to feel the love that flowed between the two subjects of the carving. Their wooden simulacra were embracing tenderly and detailed pairs of eyes gazed upon each other with obvious adoration.

Scorpion, still hugging Nathan, nodded exuberantly before planting another kiss on his blushing cheek.

The man chuckled quietly. "Well, I guess that's it. I'll go into the village tomorrow and send word for them to be collected. If the buyer is half as pleased as you are, I will be content."

The wagon for the misericords arrived four days later, just after the sun had set. Nathan was applying the finishing touches to a small statue he had been working on. "It's just a little side project," he explained to an attentive Scorpion who was curled up next to him as he applied the final coat of paint. "I just wanted to make something for you and Tigress." He smiled as Scorpion's face lit up. "Here. Have a look. Be careful, though. The paint's not yet dry."

The blonde woman leant in close and gasped as Nathan carefully placed the small statue of the Virgin and Child on his table. She turned and beckoned frantically for Tigress to come and see.

"You two have brought so much joy to my solitary life," the carver explained, his paint-smeared hands thoughtfully rubbing his cheek. "I've always lived like a hermit. Never really wanted anything to do with other people, but you two have brought sunshine to my world. So I wanted you to have this. She will protect you on your adventures."

Tigress raised a red eyebrow. "You sound like you want us to leave."

He shook his head. "No. Never. But I know your sort. You have so much adventure in your blood that you will not tarry here much longer. So, see this as a memento of your time spent here. A remembrance of me."

A silence hung in the room as an unspoken conversation passed between the two women.

Eventually, Tigress said, "Nathan, it doesn't have to be that way. You could come with us."

The man was about to reply when there was a loud banging at the door. "Ah, that must be the carter for the misericords." He heaved himself out of his chair and plodded over to the door.

It was the same man as before. The shabby-looking carter crept into the warm room. "I've come for the seats," he grunted, his eyes darting from Nathan to the women. "I've brought help."

There was a shambling clatter as six more men traipsed in and started to remove the carved priest chairs. Engrossed in their beautiful gift, Scorpion and Tigress only paid passing attention to the small talk between Nathan and the men. "I never asked where they were headed."

The carter gave a shrug that could not care less. "Some new church that's been built on a magical spring. Apparently it heals folk, if you believe that sort of thing." He stood by the fire, jabbing absentmindedly at its burning logs with an iron poker. "I just do as I am told."

The last of the misericords was loaded onto the cart. The carter gave a nod to the youngest of his companions who climbed back up behind the horses and eased the wagon away into the wood, leaving his six companions behind.

"Aren't you going with your wagon?" Nathan asked.

The carter stood up, holding the red hot poker. "Actually, we have other business before we leave."

Nathan was aware of a number of things happening at once. There was a curious noise from behind him as if someone was drawing his foot out of a wet marsh, the carter threw the poker onto the nearby bed which immediately caught fire, Scorpion and Tigress had shot across the room and, for some reason, there was a burning pain in his bowels. He looked down and saw a sharp object protruding from his stomach, covered in his blood.

Everything went grey.

The noise of transformation was unmistakable.

Constructs.

They had let their guard down and now would have to fight to save not only their lives, but Nathan's too. As they shot across the room, fangs bared and senses heightened, they saw their gentle friend slump to the floor, a bloody hole in the back of his tunic, a partially transformed construct stood over him.

That was the first one immobilised by the loss of its head.

The two vampires moved faster than the mortal eye could comprehend. They shot from one prey to another. Outnumbered, they may have been, but they were Tigress and Scorpion. Their very names poured dread into those that they hunted. One by one, bodies fell into heaps of limbs and puddles of clay as they were torn apart until, in a few minutes, five of the intruders lay incapacitated and ready for draining.

The carter remained. He stood at the door, his sullen eyes watching them. "Vile beasts," he spat, "Children of Adam and Eve's murderous son. *This* is not for the likes of you." He stashed the statue of the Virgin and Child in his jacket. "I shall put it where it rightfully belongs."

Tigress was about to leap at him when a groan came from behind.

"Yes," the carter mused, "you can try to kill me or you can save him who sheltered you all this time. The choice is yours."

The flames from the bed had already spread to the thin walls of the cottage and were starting to consume the carver's wooden creations. The vampires stood tense, desperately wanting to suck the false life out of this creature who had brought suffering to their lives, but Nathan...

"I thought so." The carter turned quickly and left the women with the bodies of his men in the growing inferno.

They needed no words. As one, the two women grabbed the gentle artist and heaved him out of the blazing cottage. The dismembered constructs would have to be left to the heat of the fire. Outside, there was no sight of the carter, nor did they expect there to be. He had disappeared into the forest and the smell of the burning building masked his vile, earthy stench.

They carried Nathan to a clear patch of grass and cradled him in their arms. Scorpion looked desperately from his deep wound to the face of her partner. Tigress looked back and nodded. "Nathan! Nathan, can you hear me?"

The dying man reached up and stroked her cold cheek. "As clearly as ever I could, my sweet Tigress, although all around me grows faint."

A drop of blood that was not his dripped onto his tunic. Tigress looked up and saw that Scorpion was crying. "You don't have to die," she said to her erstwhile saviour. "There is a way that we can save you. You can come with us.

"But it should be your choice."

A weak hand stroked feebly at her face. "No. I am finished."

More blood fell onto his torn body. This time the tears were not Scorpion's. "No, no, no..." Tigress cried, "Please. Don't. You can't. Please. Let us save you. You will be able to make beautiful things forever. Imagine that."

There was a harsh gurgle from the cooling man as he actually laughed. "That could never be, my friends. I have completed my most beautiful works and you have already completed me." His hand slowly fell from her cheek and his eyes stared off into the distance.

Tigress knelt, covered in the blood of one that she had not slain, and words failed her. She was as mute as her lover and companion who knelt with her in the deep forest, illuminated only by the burning building where they had spent a brief, wonderful time with this sweet man in his final days.

They would carry his kindness as a memento in their hearts, until the final day when they knew that their long lives would ultimately end.

They would remember him.

ABOUT THE AUTHOR

A.S.Chambers resides in Lancaster, England. He lives a fairly uneventful life for which, on the whole, he is eternally grateful as he could not be doing with any sort of day-to-day drama.

He is quite happy for, and in fact would encourage, you to follow him on Facebook, Instagram and Twitter.

There is also a nice, shiny website:
www.aschambers.co.uk

Printed in Poland
by Amazon Fulfillment
Poland Sp. z o.o., Wrocław